best wishes to the star & shadow

happy hour

sean burn

sean burn

Copyright sean burn 2012

sean burn has asserted his right under the Copyright, Designs and Patent Act 1988 to be identified as the author of this work.

This book is sold subject to the condition that it shall not, by way of trade or otherwise be lent, resold, hired out, or otherwise circulated without the publisher's prior consent in any form of binding or cover than that in which it is published and without a similar condition including this condition being imposed on the subsequent purchaser.

Published in 2012 by Skrev Press:

41 Manor Drive
HEBDEN BRIDGE
HX7 8DW
www.skrevpress.com

First Edition 2011
ISBN 978-1-904646-66-2

Cover Image: sean burn

sean burn is a writer, performer and outsider artist with a growing international reputation. he is also actively involved nationally in disability arts and was shortlisted for a dadafest disability arts award 2009. his plays are performed by breaking binary; ctc; first draft; free-thinking festival (radio three); gobscure; half moon; maverick; pegasus; paines plough; queens hall arts; under construction; weaver-hughes ensemble; zeitgeist. his thirty-plus poetry films have received many screenings worldwide, as well as at tate modern and national film theatre studios, london. he has had three spoken word cd's released, most recently speaksong (with gareth mitchell, musician). his visual poetry pamphlet (mo thunder from knives forks and spoons press) was shortlisted for the michael marks award 2011. skrev press (www.skrevpress.com) published a third full-length book of his writing (a poetry collection) – wings are giving out – (isbn 978-1-904646-56-3) in 2009.

i'd like to give a big thank you to Daithidh MacEochaidh and SKREV PRESS for their continued support for my work.

this book is dedicated to miki z

Part One	1
rabelais rules	3
moth-dreams	15
sugar and spice	24
eldorado	29
civil wars re-fought	43
balaclava'd	48
grave new world	60
gunpowder plots	64
estralita	70
lowlife	87
animal farm	91
anarcho-psychology	94
death by karaoke	97
rebecca riots and riots	103
day-tripping	106
still beating	111
part 2. those of you seeing an angel not realising it could just be a hyperactive firing of the visual cortex	112

Part One

molotovs happy hour

rabelais rules

most folks go to india to find themselves; molotov went to nicaragua to plant coffee, ended up ak47 assault rifle in hand defending the revolution. he once held off reagans terrorists for twelve hours until reinforcements came, then bandaged the wounded and cried over the dead. now he's a feral trade barista with attitude down cowl road. he's got this special deal, a nice line on a sweet sandino brew: a coffee collective from jinotega still keen to show the sandinistas gratitude. and this barista of attitude serves his brew to oxenfordes eastsiders - in the zone for independent thought but also for pretentiousness, class and cataloguings. little wonder the civil war and its beheaders lined up in this place, though defenestrations more molotovs style. he wants to keep the cowl road independent, he tries keeping it clean clean-edge.

    candide sits in the window of molotovs waiting on bootgirl - his oldest of companions. he'd wandered through three centuries until bootgirl found him cowering in a skip, bleeding slow but steady in coldcastle - the north-lands, edge of civilization, edge of land, edge. she hauled him from the rust-yellow container, he fell to the ground, staring dazed at her battle-scarred steel-toecapped purple d.m.'s, multicoloured laces wrapped back around her ankles. he named her bootgirl and she knew his madnesses, recognised his wounds, stitched his cuts this first meeting when he refused doctors, claiming they were quacks and tonic water and horse-pills, nothing more. she calmed him, got him stilled temporarily from his twitching, gyrating mind-pop - offered a brew he recognized and a settee for the night. that was years before. now way south of coldcastle, his scars are still visible, while she keeps hers well hid. bootgirls yet to finish her shift.

    bootgirl believes to this day he must-have found his-self in the pre-decimal edition of voltaire he was clutching when she hauled him from that

molotovs happy hour

rusty yellow skip, though he disputes this. that's the trouble with dissociative states, psychosis-maybe and the schizo-affective-personality disordered rest. he's been blessed with so many labels he finds it hard to remember before, though he knows it was around three hundred years ago when voltaire set him free, went off to tend his garden, gave up the big and blighted life. candide lived that volt may die, that v may have died. fragments trigger in candides mind. what were they again?

   waiting on bootgirl, waiting, only waiting, only to overhear

   - we can hardly grow vegetables in this country, how d'ya expect us to grow tea?

   yet this oxenforde is by and large tea-town, far from edgecity, coffeeville, and all the other unnameables between here and coldcastle, the edge of land, coldest place on gods earth, allegedly, though there is no god and it was a godless place, and he's thankful he's here in the middle-lands of oxenforde, of oozing river and cattle-crossing at the lowest point. the silt-flow of river past his door. the banks of thames, river yet to grow huge. and silt making the earth so rich, these layerings of history, of histories. and how this late autumn grows huge - a turning, arcing, wheeling yield of day, he wishes for a good one. for bootgirl too. waiting on her to finish her shift.

   cowl road. tales of hookers and heroin on mandala way and off the graveyard opposite. one day they cleared twelve hundred syringes out from among the tombs - apocryphal probably. watch the cctv's watching the asian tourists on their mobile-phones filming those begging for enough, just enough to score. at seven of the clock they're calling it in from the first telephone on the corner of james street, they're crying out for a twenty wrap of oblivion, or a split at a tenner each - make sure there's a crowd, make sure they each got their tenner or twenty - make sure the dealers earning enough to make it worthwhile to surf it in at eight from leys or barton or rosemund.

   blame it on that government minister über-lord mandyson strolling estates one day and hearing the huggable hoodies bang on about cooker

molotovs happy hour

hoods, not realising this was slang for the cheapest of the cheap rocks of crack, oh no he instigates a modern homes standard while in government, all council houses to have cooker hoods installed, pride and decency, proud and decent, how he likes his estates. this jewel of city - like a c.d. suspended in the breeze - is no exception.

    and at its hardest-core, a trio of sex shops porn, porn again, porn-a-go-go on this crusty, b-movie, rococo artery, jewel of a road. how do three sex shops stay in business? no-one enters. only a couple of folk come out in a day. sometimes its the same person twice. and they're never carrying anything. no briefcase, no brown envelope, not even a bulky sweater hiding skin beneath. candide has his suspicions. are they fronting something more sinister: new christianity, property speculation or human experimentation? some evolutionary psychology, social biology set-up between the university and baghdad or tel aviv? as for the newsagents of cowl road: its true transsexuals hardcore on the top-shelf of bottoms. at quickies, the window postcard offers

    attractive housewife available for massage after midnight

    beside totty's its mostly skin deep - beefcake, shaved lunk n hunk, tattoos. how these cowl road newsagents rack up cars and carmen; needle and groove; wired-up - hot and ready top-tips on twoc'ing the new mini in 60 and under. cowl road - best of all possible; worst too. its an artery that swings both ways. and like all arteries it clogs. a lorry jack-knifing to the wood yard or someone swinging out when they shouldn't - pedestrians in middle of the road in black at night; bikes bunnyhopping pavements and taking pensioners out; taxis winging it; buses on a wing-mirror and a prayer; a securicor van - its taped message blazing

    - under attack please call the police we are under attack please call

    and as for private cars, they're like buzzards looking for carrion - a right carry-on.

    a mediaeval city with twenty-first century traffic - instant infarction. cowl roads full of oxenforde buses; witney taxis; co-operative futons. but the food, the food! japanese, jamaican, indian, mexican, thai, portuguese,

molotovs happy hour

vietnamese, polish, russian, czech, chinese, malaysian, italian, french, greek and all things lebanese, syrian, turkish. cowl road brings you the world on your plate and steamed-up windows all year round en-route to work or signing on as long as you don't want serving any time soon. there's also pulse - the record shop nearby and two chemists - that's how much methadones out there.

ten past five and don't infiltrate their queueing for the cruel green unless you want

- d'ya want slicing up?

in your face and with a passion. these days set clocks to the junkie-runs, the junkie-runs, the junkie-runs. all those wanting, or needing rather, they gotta do their their taxing, their pleading, their selling and stealing by afternoon to be able to phone in for the wraps or rocks of oblivion. such easy pickings though - public school students and tourists. cowl road even has a police booth and a pissoir, the two are often confused. spills of indian, malaysian, pakistani, turkish vegetables all over pavements. sunday supplements ran how they managed to buy khat among the yards and yards of fabric. there's counselling, needle-exchange and cycloanalysts - the bike shop; there's handmade jewellery; designer rubber; dodgy computers; second-hand phones; third-hand furniture; aggressive skate-gear; more futons and porn, porn, porn until you drop – this sexxx shop is now in new hands.

take it all to heart - candide does. a litany that follows each and every new place he moves on to. finding (without looking) the sex shops within ten minutes, the red-lights, the massage parlours - you only have to walk past the life centre in coldcastle for the strip joints, meanwhile edgecity prostitutes collaborate by the station, eager to please, more eager to escape. is candide a freak radar, or just some freaked-out-radar? candide knows for sure its more than just his name. knows those two candid syllables tell all his three hundred plus years of struggling. he knows he belongs three centuries back. his place was tavern intrigues, back-stabbings, spies and chocolateering. candide knows if he's to stand any chance in the twenty

molotovs happy hour

first century he's gotta put his verbs where his periwig is. that's what voltaire wanted. those were the old-mans dying words. to spill the proverbials. spill the proverbials ol' volt said. there: between those mags should nestle a voodoo broadsheet hot on chocolate and wigging, on cut and thrust, on spy and intrigue - an inky mess of noun and adjective. voltaire-choruses it shall be named - a freewheeling tribute to the enlightenment candides constantly living through. an anti-paper, something that feels and smells of shark-skin and has a similar bite. a broadsheet of facts fantastical for the cowl road and beyond, the font is garamond, and above the mast a black and white etching of a two hundred foot periwig towering over the slumbering spires and benzo'd steeples. candides heritage snuggling the news-shelves, snug and smooth as shaved balls cupped in its authors hand. should it be priced in old coin?

candide orders another black and molotov smiles on, serving the heady brew. molotov knows its best just to smile like buddhas younger bro when candides in full-flow. candide raves on, waiting on bootgirl finishing her shift at quickies - purveyors of news and tat.

hardcore piled on to the counter of quickies, he stands, this man smelling of river-mud, twitching in pinstripes of charcoal and grey. six months shy of jesu's age when they crucified him, but all puffed up like the three days after he was crucified, silt tries blocking out those behind by pretending his shoulders are wider than they are and you're expected to smile sweetly. bootgirl don't offer an opaque bag for his porn but hands it over for all to see, she's all curtsy and

- have a pleasant and relaxing evening. sssiiir!

first lesson she learnt when fighting the narrow-minded junta of the coldlands was you gotta play it close. and bootgirls first encounter with silt is up close. soon to learn more than the smell of his mud, his thin name - lean as a pipe-cleaner, silt. there is a smell to junkies and cravers, addicts all. a smell they give off. couldn't place it at first. now she can. silt-thin mud: its always the same smell, no matter what they're on - smack, gash, cash, honey, power. the other lass refuses to serve that young property

molotovs happy hour

speculator with his silt-colored striped suit and already-thinning hair, dandruff to collar, voice wide and thin as thames at low-tide, possibly gravesend and the roll of porn - honey / petite / sweet and sour / milky mamas / someones daughter, someones nun - he's buying. no american imports but home-grown and hardcore brit wankmags - all goosebumps, appendix scars, spots over the arse and all. he must get off on the unmistakeable smell of torched body-hair, of burning pubes. it were like that back home in the coldlands way to the north. all those who kneeled to pray also preyed: pretty much all its frozen denizens asked for was a wee bit warmth. silt calls manager over, complains about bootgirls lack of craven attitude. she is sacked there and then. as the managers showing silt to the door, bootgirl pockets twenties from the till, all of them, and walks without looking back.

    bootgirl walks out into the unfurling of the muddled middlelands, having long fled the narrowed minds and prayers of coldlands northern learning. and her wean now being dreamt into existence. and on the tip of tongue all the flavours of her far-off land and knowing she cannot return; and having to make home this far-flung land that looks like thin cuts of a sad-mans arms - the wee trickle of muddy red - instead of her former cold but clear waters. here is dirty, turdy, silty. silted. muck-spread. the crap pumped into this sluggish water turned mud. oh that wanker. that wanker. that gradgrind face, thin corners of his dickensian mouth turn down - she will soon see silt more and more, and no just in her dreams. crashing through the door, through the manager, through silt she gives out wank-uuuuhh, wank-uuuuuuuuuuh, wankkkkuuuuuuuhhh hand movements and all, and all cowl road turns and follows. she feels the streets eyes as she heads to molotovs. for candide, a shoulder to cry on.

    silt. he's water off a ducks back, he thinks ugly-as-fucking, your desirable land that's out-of-luck. he see's the beauty of bricks and mortar spreading, its message of buy-buy-buy. its bye-bye to common land, allotments, green-lung. say hello concrete, hello tarmac, cheap insulation and cheaper polystyrene tiles. silts quick off the mark; he's seen the donutting

molotovs happy hour

of this former ox-crossing, the pace of folks cattle-trucking it, down-on-lucking it, moving from centre to fringes and boy will they need roofs, boy will they need roofing. he'd build on the floodplains, concrete the playing fields given half a chance. he tried for planning permission over the old leper hospital but some council fucker turned up anthrax spores. silt even bought an independent survey to say it was just mediaeval syphilis, but archaeology held its multi-layered sway, permission to build denied. least that councilman met an end: choking on swan-bone at some corporate do. no one could heimlich and so he lost the good fight. they couldn't pin anything, not a thing on silt.

the window seat is where bootgirl and candide always meet down molotovs. as connoisseurs of the heady brew, the anarchy of coffee roots plus the lack of a decent black elsewhere in this tea-town, they are well into the molotov legend. every hours happy hour as long as you drink feral trade, coffee brought back in the bags of trade unionists.

molotovs got a back court fitted with basketball hoop. the ground is glass, pure glass, sharp as his lookout. he goes out and shoots hoops each time he serves bottles of real jigger, genuine dandelion and burdock, curiosity cola, rose lemonade - that kind of. glass shot through the hoop and ... crrrrrrrraaassh. he never misses. once glass is ankle-deep he finds some fascist and persuades him to recycle all this glass, its an unofficial community sentencing. this is usually deterrent enough for them no to repeat their crimes around oxenforde. having been a racist cunt and caught by molotov and on hands and knees among a solid inch of crush and smash, plus that flat stale smell - grubbing into fascist clothes, beneath grubby bitten-off fascist nails - the stench of sweating blackshirts. they recycle, mumble, and molotov lets 'em go. they don't return. this is how he keeps it clean-edge. thames valley are always wondering why incidents of racism are so low in this wedge of oxenforde town. molotovs temper is savage. tempered only by his longing for justice.

silt prefers the anonymities of tea-house chains. their aluminium, stained-wood and terracotta walls - he wants the arteries of oxenforde,

molotovs happy hour

pumped with unfair-traded brew. his is chai, fucking impressed how you pay some stinking third worlder tuppence a day for tea leaves and then make near enough three quid by adding hot water and a leetle ambience, and still those third-worlders give thanks for your benediction. fuck! how come on those estates close to the ring road he can't see his beloved house of chai? it is the way to make a killing! he's repeatedly offered to sink some of his wad, his property money, his handyland deals into franchises of chai house for oxenfordes east-side: but so far molotovs kept him outta this patch and that's fucking silt off.

molotov may know how to handle an ak47 but silt knows how to handle a spreadsheet, bouncers, the bottom-line. excel is the new exocet. there's a war a-brewing this city where the civil war lined up. forces of republicanism versus forces of the crown. oxenforde has long been the front-line, it is the divide. in the 50's some posh northsiders built a tall wall between them and a council development, kept the godawful buggers outta sight. even the parks have ha-ha's, one side reserved for the volvo-drivers, the other, below the ditch, is for those still clinging on in the 'social' housing sector.

silts been denied in the east already. molotov and his regulars, they knew to dig deep. in the end it came down to silts outsize modern fascias breaching the listed status and etiquette of oxenforde - planning permission denied. a fragile peace. another council worker on the hit list, soon to meet his end. perhaps they should get that git morse to investigate? oh yeah he's snuffed it. was it the reverends plums in the conservatory or miss scarlet knowing how to use her length of hereditary-piping? silt reluctant at such missed riches, for now reconciled to his own landlordisms, his buy-to-let and a few extras. if silt could help, no properties would make it to open market, hell - he'd snap them for his kingdom of the expanding brownfield, greenfield, town&country waistline. what silt can't stand is people in council flats, in housing associations, in barges, in tents, under railway arches, squatting, people into settling in, those into putting their roots down.

molotovs happy hour

whats wrong with the carousel of buy, move in, do-it-up-and split-the-money with brick-man silt? he loves the whole rental market; why should some fuckers in council housing deny his fundamental rights? multiple occupancy in some streets of oxenforde runs at eighty percent. silts mission, is to drive this up by ten percent further at least and spread it south and east. so much potential, so many rooms to sub-sub-divide – he's just gotta get a few more councillors in his pocket, keep them sweet, shrink the minimum square footage, persuade health&safety to cut a little slack. the estates of barton, rosemund, leys are all within his mark-up. this is his mission. those fuckers in rosemund, barton, leys who are still in council property - he wants syringes in the streets until they are forced the fuck out and he mops up. oh sweet, yeah. those anti-social fuckers in social-housing they are such a denial of his fundamentals. war is coming, silt reckons. property rights. he wants to get his teeth right the way in.

he don't get cowl road. why does it have to stay independent? rebel against the laws of market, the law of build? but the time is coming, the time is coming, silt feels it like the tide, feels the concrete, knows its about to floweth, yea, a war is coming, a real walls, floor and roof guerre of our times; and silt sees his-self in beret and bovver boots, the biggest, the mostest, über-weapon to hand, directing his irregular army into slash and barnstorm. then cream over molotovs and sweep out the indie coffee-stakes for franchised tea.

his ultimate passion - some would say curse - is to explore another imported substance - young and foreign flesh for massage parlours with all the extras, all the trimmings. this is what they call synergy in business-world. he takes leonard cohens give me crack and anal sex as a command. reckons he can get the programme up to speed, make a killing, and how. for now he holds in mind - his temporary east-side defeat. there's another mark on his sheet. another set of names he gotta defeat ... nurses it with a mug of nameless big chain xxxploitation. silt is addiction personified. he is the narco-wet dream. dandruff still in place on his collar, getting thicker and he, he still can't get enough of bright young things in cocaine sex, anal

molotovs happy hour

bricks&mortar, the bright red virtuoso porn-slaughter of property to let, of mortgages and the virtual, virtuoso, viral market, of handshake and close.

   oh blood-banker, estate agent of the future – he's got it bad. if he's not closing, if he's no pushing - pushing up the price, pushing the language, pushing the angles - if he's no driving round with someone elses keys - he starts to shake. his pens permanently unsheathed. ink is his middle name. sometimes it covers his middle-pocket. and just like ink - he wont wash-out. sometimes he lets his-self into a property early just so's he can jerk off - mind where you step, and if you stick to the lino, well! he loves leaving his sweet sweat - an invisible rime around. one time he was caught almost, but silt prides his-self on being quick to cum. and boy is he! his current lady-loves a thirties house with all original features. its in the south of the city, and is rising by a hundred and fifty a day. he's got to get over there double-quick. silts mobile is a loaded weapon. his car-keys are go. his zipper is greased. and now there's a sub-standard end-of-terrace build at bottom-end of the same southern estate as well and still he's gonna flog it for two hundred thou, plus. most of its cheap timber, the sparrows have managed to crack their way in and are nesting in the attic, though silt is gonna have them boarded up and in, let 'em rot, he'll close quick - once the wee winged corpses start to stink its no his problem. he hasn't had this much fun since sunday school and all that he loved to do for the nice preacher-woman to earn his extra sweet. crack and anal sex: how her number came up. but now its his that rings and rings and rings.

   candides sick and tired of another white v.w. splayed across what passes for drive these parts of his estate, just off rosemunds oval. so tired he is of all this twoc'er sprayed glass, he's filled the earth outside the garage he squats and calls home, with spikes pointing upwards to take out those tyres, working his this'll teach the fuckers into remaining spaces of ground, so tired candide is of it all. he's embedded green glass, brown glass, clear and blue glass into the ground around. wine bottles - red and white and rosé; french wine, chilean wine, even new zealand. polish gherkins, english

molotovs happy hour

pickled onions, german sauerkraut. jam, marmalade and fruit jellys. mostly fished from others recycling bins. their glasscrush spikes instead of grass, aye candides tired alright, and now car-fucked near-enough. it stopped just before landing in what passes for his living room, bedroom, kitchen – this single garage. toilets the wall outside. as for bog paper: last weeks book review in-case the poet laureate or their mates are featured. the lounge is the settee out-front salvaged from a local skip, a tarpaulin over to keep off the rain. this garage is candides secret. his and ashes. this is where they crashed having fled together that hospital overlooking the killing moors of edgecity. oh yes. shipman, hindley, brady, and sutcliffe the yorkshire ripper - they haunted those moors above edgecity. perfect place to site an asylum. ash said he had wings, candide claimed to be three hundred, most patients just claimed to be a god. all the psychiatrists truly believed they were god.

ash and candide - they crashed out, flew south, passing through tamworth at about three a.m. how all routes pass through tamworth eventually. car they'd taken got them to the oxenforde bypass where it gave out. ash and candide kept walking. knew if the psychiatric spies were out looking they would expect candide / ash to approach from the north. so they kept on round the ring road, approaching from the south. found rosemund. found an unused garage. it seemed like eldorado. and there they squatted. and there they are to be found still. no doubt silt could get sixty grand for this garage. instead ash and candide got busy, got lino, a wee gas stove, stove-top espresso maker. they crap in carrier-bags.

candide can't be arsed calling for the crashed car outside to be cleared. besides it adds camouflage. and who to call? council does fuck-all and in these parts no even that, save those taking backhanders and passing the dodgy land-grabs through. besides they'd have to pay council tax on this squat if the council found out. this is home, sort-of, for now. bootgirl got the message, flew south too. now there's three who don't fit in these strange and strained middlelands, southlands really – bootgirl, ash, candide. and their bodyguard – molotov. someones written with marker pens to the

molotovs happy hour

twisted white v.w. - and dick loves cunt and cunt loves dick and dick loves dick so dial 07957-40343. and voltaire enjoyed his ménages à trois and the church below and the sky above and you gotta laugh, keep teary ducts from freezing; and out candides car-battery-powered one speaker - a jazzy overture the best of all possible worlds.

    all this ringing out as sunset wraps itself round the thinnest of land. all warp and no weft, all vein, no artery, all pumpkin, no coach or horse, hammer, no tongue - you know how the story of this place goes. and somewhere in it all: star-gloried, molotov showing bootgirl how to close up for the evening, he's taken her on straight away on hearing her news. she's to crash at his, no point in staying alone out on the leys, no. molotov'll get her up mornings to unlock and help him out in the coffee shop.

    candide walks slowly down cowl road, along boundary brook, up rosemund and home. there in eldorado he waits on ash, who is no doubt in full flight, somewhere. off romney place some fuckers sprayed rabelais rules!

    candide sinks into the heaviness, and waits

moth-dreams

ash: how he got his name is this. sitting there, the moorlands loon-bin. summer storm heading over the moors, passing edgecity, heading for ash, heading for him, looking for his skin. the beat-beat-repetitive, of rain. the slap / dash of wind. ahead of it all moths came a-flocking. moths flocked, ahead of that dark, outrunning storm. moths they came off moors, off rushes, off heather and bilberry. moths – small, medium, impossible - they flocked, outpacing storm. ash sits expectant. knowing this would happen. he knew. the moths settling on him as he looks out window onto that gathering storm. the moths in their millions settle to his dark skin shrouding and around. moths. moths. moths. even the psychiatric nurses going what the fuck as moths settle all over ash. all clothed in moth he is. all moth he is. their wing-beat so many r.p.m., he is covered with their pale moon ash, as they take shelter from the storm, and he sits zazen as zen, silent and still, cloaked in moth, forbidding the nurses from batting at him. nurses finally quieten for the night as storm subsides and moths disperse from off his skin back to the moorland, their dark shadows leaving edgecitys moorland psychiatric establishment.

   ash rode out the storm, moth clothed. and candide watched ash. and in the morning candide wakes him with the crud they call coffee, three sugars, everyone knows its decaf really, sweepings, dregs they hide in normal jars, the last patient to complain got locked in i.c.u, returned to the ward three weeks later minus their front teeth. as candide wakes him, ash is clothed all over with moths ashy powder shimmering, translucent, iridescent, like oil across water. his skin has taken this on as a new layer that don't settle but moves and flows. candide reaches, tentatively touching. the puddlings of tiny scales mosaic away from his finger. they flow like liquid rorschach. oh boy the psychiatrists gonna be pleased. candide produces a long leather trench coat from one of his shoplifting adventures.

ash pulls this on. now ash hides his skin, keeps the trench coat on, wont let it off from now on. ash, candide says, we gotta call you ash.

ash has a recurring dreaming. sands so hot from global warming, and through this glass at his feet the last remaining eroded blocks of stone from coldcastle, now mostly beneath sands or wave. we are a thousand years in the future and ash sees his-self slowly walking across those sands. there is a heat-haze and a blur and a shift. and a southern diplomat at a table in the vast sands. ash approaches this seated diplomat.

- passport

ash produces an orange.

- passport

ash places this orange down.

- passport!

ash produces a knife. diplomat stiffens. ash opens blade. diplomat sweats. ash cuts orange in two, he hands over half to the diplomat, sucks his own half. after this dream ash wakens smiling, still in his long leather trench coat, the music on his lips. he moves from the light of sleep to the darkness of days.

ash got moved to the outskirts of coldcastle after his mother flew. whitest place. and he, dark as the sea-coal he danced among in a coldcastle-white world, and his foster-mam, she laughed - and though they were white and he was black - he thought it must be something to do with the coal - he thought it was literally that rubbing off, turning his skin different, that's what he thought. however time has meant he has learnt his black is to live. learnt from within. learnt he wasn't those hating names ... learning what he was. now he understands, heading south - loud as dock-cranes, nifty as a sand-dancer, mouth wide-open as the foghorns all down the coast - he thinks this must be why folks stare. only then meeting candide in the moorland hospital and all that moth business and candide the only one not staring and that cemented their friendship in ashes hollowed-out world. ashes secret: he is preparing for flight.

by contrast candide occasionally dreams his lips sewn shut. candide

molotovs happy hour

gave up all other dreams aeons ago. three hundred years of dreaming is too many. most nights he is sleepless, lipless, sometimes eyeless, never legless. this night might be the amytripline. they have decided he is ill, yeah - his mad melts like clock/s; but chronic, chronic-o. candides rouged lips are singing antidepressants and anti-psychotics both. he lies there exhausted, rolls over, pulling the duvet stolen from another skip off ash who wakes his skin feeling the quicksilver of those repetitive moth wings, a gift to him, one good turn deserving another. ash can feel his-self flexing, soaring, feels his winged-self preparing for the long long haul. together they fire up the gaz – hit the brew.

silts dreamless. he sleeps so fucking well. ain't it always the way. who says crime don't pay? choose bastardy and you sleep like a babby. choose honesty, or have innocence choose you and you'll be sleepless, twisting, gurning, all over this world. silts nights are dark, a void. avoid.

molotovs dream. a mural. winged. esteli. matagalpa. jinotega. the north always, north nicaragua. this is why he went. knew it was destined. that mural in his mind before he knew how to spell managua. when he saw nicaraguan folk-art pictures he knew it for a message, a sign. they had the same colour, tone, line as his dream, his dreaming. a folk-mural on walls: one of the few left over from sandino perhaps? and there, there on these house-end paintings are winged beings, winged folk, a peasant version of bosch or chagall, stretching their feathered beings alongside the non-winged folk. molotov salutes them, shoulders his weapon, ploughs on.

bootgirl dreams the play of her life. a tight spotlight on her unmoved, unmoving face as one by one the characters process. doctor enters slaps left side of face. bootgirl doesn't twitch. defeated, doctor leaves. teacher enters. slaps right side of her face. bootgirl don't twitch. defeated, teacher leaves. soldier enters, strikes stiffly both sides her face. no twitch. soldier departs. and now a procession of representatives of her coldlands and its regime pass. diplomat, clown, priest, driver, artist, caretaker, librarian, driving instructor, clock-gazer, card-turner - all entering, slapping, leaving, defeated.

molotovs happy hour

ash dancing fills candides mind. its an escape from the here and now - a place candide has little in common with and less love for. how could someone so black, so beautiful, dance so camp? candides never put it to ash. suspects it might be racist but it plays his mind. over and over. dancing. it might be only dancing but down corridors that asylum it looked like his shadows taking flight and when ash told his innermost secret that he was hollowing out and preparing to fly candide didn't blink once. ash in a world of his own, ash is in.

now they're safe in oxenforde they dance the zodiac nights away. some nights molotov is there weaving an ak47-stripdown-clean-reassemble dance of hands. bootgirl stomping an eternity on the face of the regime in her purple d.m.'s. together they make a beat, a pulse, ferocious, not to be denied. candide knew its real cos cath carroll was singing, playing, all dancing, and carroll, she swells, all brazilian percussion, bass, and miaow-voice on how england made her.

the psychiatrist and his hangers-on have refused to meet molotov in outpatients. they want him in the main body of the kirk so to speak, pull down the engaged signs on the nearest door, these days they even have security standing by – course it might just be some geezer locked up for liking uniforms but that looks unlikely, they have i.d. badges. and even with security the psych doesn't like to start on candide until he's been half risk-assessed to death. anyways this is the last chance saloon - it has the mock versailles furniture - they're right fuckers to hurl through windows. candide told the crash-team, his alternatives-to-admission or a2a as the c.p.n.'s are so trendily re-branded - he is, really is three hundred years old plus and out pages voltaire. that was last time they caught him, caught up with him, now three days on he hasn't heard fuck-all yet.

he checks cars parked outside to see if they're in hiding, waiting ready to section. he explained to social work how this land is filled with advanced animatronics, most people aren't – they're puppets, you can see if you look close. trouble is they're programmed to respond once you do. candide looks close. they responded. candide knows all this about anima-

molotovs happy hour

tronics and puppetry is true though. that's how the cloned beings in this place are rich. they don't need to buy food, only a tiny amount of rubberised fluid and oil keeps them running. singing, dancing in oxenforde seems somehow apt. and candide made a right song and dance. there's more musicians per square inch than any other city - or was that therapists per square inch? music therapists possibly. some nights its orchestra wars - rivals out fly-posting but oh so nicely. cellos at dawn. oboes at three paces. chronic not psychotic - the judgement. but this is a fine-balance that could so easily swing the other way. always the first question how you sleeping? he hates psychiatrists saying
- this will help you
hates psychoanalysts asking
- why do you think this would help?
hates psychologists asking
- help, help? but would it?
hates the doctor asking
- would it help?
the music therapist wheezing with their accordions
- what would help in b flat?

he especially hated the photocopier attendant asking, asking, asking. all he wanted was an a-bloody-three copy for a trial run of voltairechoruses. ended taking the copy-shops hammer to his own good-wrist until bloodied but unbowed it fermented, purple, yellow, the radius chipped. d'ya have any idea how much strength it takes to bust your own bones in public? that's where they caught up with him. he don't want back in hospital. they don't want him in, not really. they want the nice cases, the easy-peasy ones. they didn't go into psychiatry for blood!

what candide does know is that after all the hullabaloo, the brouhaha, shortly after all that he was in ashmoles museum wearing a periwig and dancing a saltarello, one arm in a bloody sling. his inspiration was the million pound stradivarius they got locked up, the finest ever made so it is said, only - their words - its too valuable to be played. an instrument

molotovs happy hour

locked in a case can't be right so candide gave a little dance to cheer it up. the strad seemed to be smiling though the attendant queried this. candide, he blew the dust off ol' ashmole, what dusty company he keeps. ashmole striking thirteen, candide skipping outta old ashmoles place, dusty but happy, until the sneezing dust-fever hits, and he is gigging up and down chronic again. when the touristos came in from their buses of beaumont street or saint giles he told them he's living history, reliving history, dancing a saltarello for the poor caged violin; they applaud the re-enactment, what fine museum education. candide didn't get further, blue-lights moved in and candide moved on.

to the randolph. its where that murderer churchill dined. his gravy stains are there still. picture candide trying to get into the randolph in full gear, powdered bosom, corset à la claphouse - with a tied periwig - you know the sort with a ponytail at the rear, very fashionable, v. eighties - sixteen eighties that is. louis going bald, commissioning a wig, and all the courtiers thinking this was such a great trend they bewigged theirselves and the craze spread across europe, no good candide should be without one and when asked who he is: candide explains he's part of a living history exhibition over the road at ashmoles. its called outreach - the latest thing. he camps it up, gives more ham than keanu reeves jockstrap. oh. they say, oh. and go to let him in winstons fave eatery.

only to have police catch their slippery customer and whiz him uphill to the victorian centre for deranged gentlefolk as it was titled then, or the ford-wars hospital as it now is. top consultants debate whether he's a danger, they don't connect him to that previous moorland unit – can't find the notes under c for candide, must-of been misfiled, plus candide couldn't really be charged with wearing a periwig during daylight hours, specially as this time he has his frock-coat on - so no real obscenities and no damage done. candides more concerned with why periwigs are not everyday attire throughout this oxenforde. candides confused wandering the b roads of this city; seeking out the wearers of periwig and finding none. he even asks the officers where are the wigs but they thought he was insulting the judi-

molotovs happy hour

ciary and warned him off.

half-hour earlier the coppers were all being treated by silt. candide didn't know silt were in – knowing to look out for his face after bootgirl had warned them all about that fucker who got her sacked. all candide remembered was police parking up on the pavement, getting out with their toolman belts, cuffs, cs spray, extendable dildo-cum-batons, radio, battery backup, mobile phones to scramble the crooks scanners and all. earpiece looked over to him, looked him over, compared notes with the other bluebottle, but they move in and upstairs and candides left outside as they had more urgent things to attend to. he continues his dance for the violin of violins and now they're finally getting round to asking his address. he gives out rosemund. older of the coppers rolls eyes, younger 'un offers to drive. they let candide off by the turn into the estate. any further and they'd no be welcome. they've lost three cars in there in recent weeks as it is.

they called out the alternatives to admissions team, gave candides details, rolled back down to the safety of skinny-chai streets, of impossible pink skies, pink painted walls, the salmon stone of city centre oxenforde, and cherry trees, plum trees, apple trees – why is the fruit allowed to rot? candide gets shouted at when he tries eating it. and a2a - alternatives to admission - don't like hitting rosemund either, the junkies think it really is eldorado – raid their vehicle for all the available uppers, downers, antipsychotics, painkillers, syringes – the best of all possible worlds, oh yeah.

autumn: season of mists and all that shite. autumn: the pulse of fruit, fruit dropping, fruit hitting the gutters. fruit oozing and fermenting down drains. autumn fruit: the perfect naked image of this place. plum trees, damson trees, pears, apples, crab-apples, medlar, red cherry, black cherry, mulberry, even nectarine trees for christsake! gardens full. parks full. verges full. common and uncommon land full. private and not so – the branches hung low over pavements inciting a fruity riot. only. only ... what do the good-folks of this place do? they buy sealed polybags from chile, france, new zealand, and leave the free fruit to drop and rot. told to eat five pieces a day as your patriotic duty. and some do. only not this islands

molotovs happy hour

free fruit, no, bought fruit is what gets eaten. and anyone out there harvesting the free fruit gets stared down, shouted down, run down. cars parked on pavements to prevent people from getting close. climb on the bonnets my friends, reach your hands up, reach up. hell, they've got trees bearing fruit you can't even buy down those same stores. fruit in the gutter. this is no metaphor, it is no simile, it is actuality. the perfect, useless, perfumed crash and fall of this place. where else but oxenforde? mouths like plums. vowels like damson. and the sting of loganberry heels.

    candides thankful that autumn and winters honest about its coldness. he hates spring. loathes its false optimism. candide hates those days when you just know the animatrones, the puppet-subjects, replicants all, of these streets will be out all night, applying pink tissue-paper blossoms on all the trees to cheer up commuters, make 'em think its all ok, when it aint. go on. look close at the trees. look closer. you can see its paper and glue. watch out when it rains. gutters fill with tear-sodden paper hankies of blossom. street-cleaners trudge and de-sludge, cyclists get covered in the cack, and drivers try and hit it ... spray up this mock floral sewage over the pavement-walkers. oh yeah the drivers love broadsiding it just so. tree-dressings are only so many lockerbies, candide knows, he sees and sees through it all.

    the c.p.n.'s - community psychiatric nurses - actually respond to the coppers call-out to attend candide. they actually penetrate rosemund. big burly fuckers so they are, used to giving it back. c.p.n.'s ask if he has any strange or weird thoughts and then wonder why he laughs. its a roundabout big as the london road. behave yourself. take your tablets. keep your appointments. be a good boy. its been like this for years. at least they didn't have psychiatrists in the eighteenth century - another plus, one more good thing from candides yoof - but it don't feel good to him. he reminds hisself to look up the word pompadour. it nestles between polyphagous and peyote. candide can't explain those feelings of what he believes must be normality and which come each time he lets his blood. it don't hurt, not in the least. besides blood-letting was an enlightenment cure. candide con-

molotovs happy hour

templates his fate. and now though he's explained his woes, here in his garage squat he's made to sit and they force on him a paper cup (no sharp edges) and water, watch him swallow, swallow all, swallow it down, and he's told, told yeah, he gotta swallow it all - he gotta pay attention, he gotta behave, he gotta take the medication, keep his appointments or else - it will be secure unit for you - no more night-times thinking we can't see, no more taking different routes to outdo surveillance, no more pissing us around. candide bows his head. knows they mean it. its a battle now. its war. he gotta stay smarter than them, he gotta keep one step ahead

molotovs happy hour

sugar and spice

looking for talent in this place? its no hard. sculpted boys, eager girls - androgynes in cycle-shorts even in january and all their tallow-flesh public-schooled or alt.scene enough to swing both ways and most with accents to turn you wild yet simultaneously keep your hard-on at bay

   - of course maman supplies all my water. she's driving down with another fortnight even as we speak

   sitting in molotovs, bottom of cowl road, gazing and grazing on talent flooding the pavement outside, though all of a look-but-don't-touch kind, and mostly of a rugby top kind and predominantly of a home counties trofimov; they'll shag provided you're mad or homeless or seeking asylum or dreadlocked enough. its good for their soul, letting a little class consciousness in. end of the day its all about a bit of rough - your mistake would be to settle down with any these fuckers.

   bootgirl very nearly did settle for one of these fuckers: one of her none-too-rare mistakes of the loving kind. her problem is she still sees only the best in folks. soft-hearted, listening, she hasn't learnt to go yeah, yeah, yeah - she still has much to learn. and now left with a wee black and white photo from the ratcliff hospital of this tadpole, picture that could be runner-up in amphibious weekly, her babby looks like a newt. she wishes she could give sex up but it feels so good until all comes unstuck, again and again and again.

   ash and candide cruise every so often, mostly for a laugh. these days however they plot and plan voltairechoruses - this place is so ripe for broadsheets, sedition, anti-establishmentarianism. bootgirl will be along after the prenatal scan - if the number ten bus can be arsed running back from the ratcliff hospital. ash and candide they're talking up voltairechoruses a storm to mol – how this broadsheet could brew sedition and take the rip to bankers street, merchant strasse, property boulevard, yeah.

they're up for printing a broadsheet of unpalatable facts about this place, paste these pages up on willing walls and let the people judge this city where civil war lined up.

    candide first took ash cruising outside the old dairy of headington hill park - lots of shrubs, campus close by - fools on the hill the other university calls them, but they're just jealous ... anyways this is the place to be - not that he gets much luck - i mean who'd want a fat old both-ways sweaty, not exactly appetizing - and he don't cottage as such, mostly its window shopping: its more about the adrenalin, the fear. in the past he hoped to become hiv positive, years when he wanted to get ill, be sick, a slow suicide - felt he deserved it, so tired with his centuries on this lump of rock.

    he's past that mostly - though he does go to these places now and again. walk across to saint clementines, walk up headington hill, fail to pull, fail to get bashed just - walk away weak-legged - adrenalin racing like this is the most he's lived; like a triple shot of caffeine. voltaire showed candide how to swing. those ménages à trois, fours, fives! was a time when condoms were made out-of goats or sheep intestine. a time when nothing was wasted. candide licks lips. but ash – well when they all see glorious, gobsmacking, magnificent him, in long leather coat, they see some cinema hero, nero, somesuch. be p.c. as you want but when someone like ash makes his entrance - p.c. goes out the window; you all - and i mean all - turn your heads, a little ball of spittle involuntary leaving corners of mouth. each and everyone turns into a raging queen - even the hetero'est of the hets start whimpering, even the bullest-dykes call him butch. and once you see what he is made of, its all sugar and spice and all things m-mmm-mmmmm.

    the way candide gave ash head made him laugh; they've been friends ever since - having made a promise to never sleep with each other again - other than just sharing a bed. well they did once candides jaws had stopped aching from wrapping themselves round that, that thing - you know how it is when you get that godawful cocksuckers cramp. so yes they remained good friends candide and ash.

molotovs happy hour

   three lads hanging over in molotovs far corner with two lasses - all are wearing pube-line jeans. candides watched belt lines getting lower, lower. in austens day it was around your tits, by gertrude stein it was hung lower, by kathy acker bellybuttons were on display, but these are the first pubes on display. no trim. no neatness. but a luxuriance ... like the shrubbery, the cottaging, frottaging shrubbery, laurel crown of the park of earlier. those pube-line lads and lasses are joking, chatting, txting. candide can't get his head round the weirdness of txting. especially not when you're txting the person you're right next to - as they are. lads heads turn to this lass walking past the window, muscular, taut, boyish. now she's entering the door. lads turn back,
  - you better tighten up yer act girls.
   lasses turn to each other, couple their arms through, give the v's, walk off. bootgirl enters and turns to admire the swing of the lasses arses thinking atta girls. the lads turn to her, any words on their lips freeze on realising she is way outta their league. hers are strictly seven league boots.
   bootgirl sits. molotov smiles. she smiles back. she asks again why ash doesn't take his trench-coat off. he never does. candide leans over and whispers confidentially – he doesn't want to show off his wings. bootgirls used to dealing with psychosis, but sometimes it catches her still. molotov slides a cappuccino over, she smiles and molotov thinks her smile is the moon. everyone's smiling. its like return of the zombies. candide wonders why there's always silvered crescents of spit - wee globs of dried-out toothpaste - down his front. is it his tongue-piercing? back then they did it with skewers. candide may be a messy bugger - unable to spit fully due to that cumulative weight of metal in his mouth but say what you like, it does allow for fun. candide thinks the comtesse of fellatio and duc de cunnilingus may have been at court during old voltaires reign? candides not fussed so long as there's some kinda flesh to wrap his wee knob of metal around. a special place. its special special tricks. oh yeah. tonguing. tongue-in.
   if anything happens to me you get to inherit my air-hostess barbie -
   latest graffiti in molotovs bogs. they suspect molotov wrote it up his-

molotovs happy hour

self just in case any fascists were looking to take a piss. ash and candide say they gotta go collect this letter press they've begged of freecycle. now they've found how to print their broadsheet voltairechoruses, its all moving forward. molotov comes over to chat with bootgirl. he wants to know about the babby, its on his mind. she thinks he'd make a good co-parent but blushes at her thought. molotov likes when she does that. it flips pancakes in his mind.

- i wouldn't dishonor buses by bringing a fag on them

it really was said on the number three - as in fascist haircut - bus heading south, all the way to rosemund. the fag-baiting of candide and ash, even though they're both bi. those dickheads on the bus and their cruddymouths, plus their longing to sink the blade in. their nastinesses, all those words - shirtlifters / benders / bumboys / shit stabbers / fucking vaseline freaks. candide pushes the stop button, stands up, and before getting off, turns to the butchest lad

- next time you're bent over taking it up the ass i'd advise a water based lubricant – unless you wanna be torn apart

zits across butches face look like lamb-fat on the hospitals hotplate, overheating, sizzling, like they're gonna explode, something even gargantua would turn up his nose at. candide and ash leap off opposite the rosemund chippie where the teenagers carry out their the rituals of i'm going with her / you're dumped / i'm going with him / she's a slapper / you've got no balls / tight-arse / lezzer / one inch dick.

with bootgirl all this never was an issue. sure there'd been men but that was mostly like d.i.y. without the sore-wrists until the right woman came along. yeah there were a few men, sometimes, if she was randy enough she'd go for men, but penises make her laugh. cock. prick. dick. meat thermometer. little soldier. wanger. schlong. enlarged-clit. her mistake was getting pregnant. now she's expecting, she longs to be held, not fucked, but a man could do, maybe, you know ... she blushes more as molotov nods his head. takes his mind off the sold signs either side his coffee house, takes his minds off requests to meet silt and discuss terms to settle up move on before the nastiness starts. meanwhile under gay in the local guides it says - see train station, bus station, head london, head any-which-way, only head. this candide and ash decide amounts to what will form the queer-corner of their voltairechoruses broadsheet - advising queers of all persuasions to see train station, bus station, head anywhichway, only head. did freud ever lecture here? oxenforde is a sphincter held tight

molotovs happy hour

eldorado

set your clock these days by the addicts needing their eight p.m. fix. ringing it in and then collecting at eight as they always do from the phone box right below the carfax tower. it sure does clear the streets. soon as bells chime eight, everyone else puts their head down, jumps in a taxi, jumps a bus, melts, melts away. did pavlov teach classical conditioning in this wedding cake? bells toll and you run from the ghosts of heroin ringing it in. no-one cruises the bus station bogs off gloucester green anymore: you're gonna get someone needing to shoot-up right now, and busting the door in: even the thames valley coppers have put in needleboxes. if you're off a country bus and needing a shit, hold it in - you've no chance; there's a fine mist of blood on walls - like holding your hand over a hose until fine spray gives out - some addict hitting an artery instead of a vein; happens all the time. when will someone privatise the ambulance services? they could make a killing.
 this corner below the carfax tower happens to be the perfect place for dog-ends. the number one bus always arriving just as they're firing up – one old lad has worked it to perfection, collecting fags that are almost whole. fights have been known to happen – blood-spill over the implausible quality of tobacco on these soured streets, and that's just the centre. but this place adrift, this middle-lands of merry old albion, of morris-dancers and apiarists, of actuaries and bell-ringers, of philosophy lecturers and wing-resetters, of period-instrumentalists and light light-engineers, they don't get it. can't see beyond their patios. addiction is the same whether you're a white knuckle drunk ex-president, some smackie off the peripheries, or a northsider stiff with gout, fixing another port and wondering just how much his first edition of the bayreuth programme is worth. a drug is a drug and an o.d. is still an o.d.. yes a drug is a drug and an o.d. is still an o.d. whether you're a lass whose done too many paracetamols

molotovs happy hour

over-anxious about cello-lessons, sats or possibly over the way her dads suddenly started leering and she's started locking the bathroom door, or you're sunk in a doorway with a schizophrenic for brother, another for father, and a mother whose done a runner, and you've always been called trouble. no, an o.d. is still an o.d., and a cut is still a cut. whether you're fifteen and your long-sleeved slipknot top covers the carving lines on your arms, or a twenty-something, pierced belly, nice maori-tat on your right shoulder kind of a gal whose cut open her belly, or a three hundred year old psychotic, losing your memory in the ford-wars hospital, a cut is still a cut, and a scar is always a scar.

and a place to live is a home not a property investment, not a development opportunity, not a gladrags to riches story. it is not an excuse to make more homeless if they don't fit your profile. but the places to live have all been sold-off. and the streets are paved with a rosy light as it bounces off mediaeval walls just so ... and an order to move on and drink your kestrel, buckfast, or beg less aggressive because of the tourists, yes a public order offence is still a public order offence. stiffed and stuffed and raise a glass, drink good health, ignore the o.d.'s, ignore the cuts, raise your drawbridges even while leaving the curtains open onto drawing-rooms just so others can see all the costly stuff they're missing. look leather-bound volumes, look original art, look art-deco vases with english gladioli, look edible gold-leaf, look futon-throws, look bowls of organic starfruit and physalis, look his and hers driveways. don't look addiction up but do look up to your diction – all elongated syllables. it is you oxenforde, ye olde class-divide and rule where the civil war lined up, you are spawning this. this is your progeny, you are tripping over your own ovums, slipping on your own sperm.

sociologists and psychologists can do as much action-research and pilot studies into social drift hypothesis and relative deprivation theory as they like but these middle-lands are laying their own future, and still you don't get it. fuck and birth, wonder and despair. look: first editions. look: art signed by the artist. look cello lessons in the nude. why don't you look to

molotovs happy hour

the fifty pound note up your nose – whose face does it feature, whose bloodstains are those? look depression, repression, insurrection. look repressed homosexuality and english hubbies and un-t.v.-tubbies available for massage after midnight, english-rose wife approves and may look on. look classical orchestras, look ketamine, look eating disorders, self-harm and overdosings. look shares in pedigree greyhounds, look mummy, daddy, i'm going to the dogs. look at the spacewagons parked on your pavements and the dog turds jostling with dog-ends for space in the gutter, alongside the homeless and the psychotic. and why hasn't this saint petersburg-on-thames become gramscigrad? you have enough linguists surely? why aren't you twinned with ho-chi-minh city? why haven't you presented this terms paper on insurrection, and please ensure it is correctly footnoted this time. look another museum of modern art rebranded, reframed, reprinted, re-arranged, refrained, retrained, detained, replanted, regraded and retrograded. mao sprayed up your walls. look cultural revolution, look peasants, look. just don't expect anyone to meet your eye.

    silt met meatman over a bag of pork-scratchings in the king of prussia one night during an england qualifier. meatman knocking off from delivering his organic smoked meat specials out-back-of his customised van. he runs his business from his beloved hitlermobile - covering north oxenforde, wolvescoat, whiter-park - and the opera villages of grassing-you-upton and beyond. so pleased is he with organic-business, its added value, he pays a tithe to the home-counties nazi collective, at least the english defence league have guts, the b.n.p. didn't stand in these parts, spineless. and silt: silt letting down his shirtsleeves from the rosemund estate agents - his personal eldorado - where property is happening, trade mark awaited.

    - c'mon my son. c'mon. 'ave 'im. 'ave 'im

    silt and meatman both cheering on a nutting of the opponent, so saint george. they united over violence on the pitch, over crowded pints and above all over meatmans special bags of limited edition pork scratchings. aye, their bonding was over pig-strips – and then a confession for smokies

molotovs happy hour

– sweetmeat sheep burnt and scorched, blow-torched. smokehouses may be illegal, but oh so sweet. silt tells how alongside properties he can offer personalised coats of arms and baronetcies bought-up cheap from the bankrupted. meatmans going to take him up on a coat of arms for his van in exchange for a quantity of smokies, hell yeah.

beware the prick beneath soles of feet, the crunch of needle-spikes. play-parks full. oh sure, what makes this place so bleeding-special - why shouldn't they have the same as coldcastle or edgecity, a market is a market. why shouldn't it rise like a roller-coaster, ascend to a price sweeter than heaven, serenaded by fat-slag seraphim, pornstar cherubim. core and periphery. core and periphery. someones writing their p.h.d. thesis on this even as we speak. the core just get their drugs less cut is all.

silt can't resist spilling to his new found mate how he's piling the pressure on cowl road. he's bought out those either side of molotovs. didn't the new age wiccan witch next door see that one coming in her crystal balls? he even pressurised rubber specialists the other side to relocate just by tightening their nipple clamps that extra degree. they weren't expecting quite so much pain. burn-out on the peripheries means twisted metal, the odd art student taking photographs, hoping to get a first. on the leys there's a crackhouse opposite the local m.p. - no-one ever accuses him of no inhaling, or of not backing war – a war, any war. soon the arms-dealers'll be setting up shop, sponsoring oxenforde colleges. oh yeah, they have. silt wants their m.b.a..

silt bites through four layers bread, two beef and dripping - eating the two sandwiches as one. he always does: saves time. time for for closing, for wanking, for gravy, or for trouble in a crowd. soon there's to be a new delivery of vietnamese. delightful. so girlish. no tits - some of them, nipples only. one of silts multi-occupancy sidelines is housing some of these 'imports' who offer massage with all the extras. costs shedloads to bring one into the country these days: border patrols, sniffer dogs, heat-seeking cameras, bribes to pay, cctv to be turned the other way - there's outlay before they're even working. and once they are – there's h&s to pay off, councillors to turn the other way, police to turn away, discrete marketing and astronomical phone-bills. if they want to work here, they gotta pay - and if they wanna argue well whose to say how their severed torsos got into the thames. there's a hundred-plus navigable miles below here - they could-of got in anywhere - that's a hell of a lot of water.

once one of those cute-teenies couldn't wrap her alien-tongue around silts name, called him slit: she didn't again. so that one was a waste of cash as he cut her in front of the other imports, explaining this is what slit meant. he used meatmans best knife-set - a gift in return for frequent flier status with the girls. they learnt to hold their tongue, honour silt, as he and meatman took the carcass, its nothingness, flopped it to the late-night waters somewhere around henley. a dogwalker in richmond got an early morning surprise days later. in death – unlike life – she made the local news, nothing more. home-office had a spokesperson het under the collar about these bloody immigrants, economic migrants all, when will they learn? and that was that. yardies are the number one problem right now according to the chief constable. yardies around oxenforde means those without proper patios: poor dears.

silt is proud to be english - ah the good rich soil - silt flows through the river-veins; slit is what he makes to spill his salt into. silt loves nothing better than to masturbate into the fresh wounds of others. him and meatman circle-jerking in front of that fresh delivery of yellow-beauties who quickly learnt to keep their mouths shut. that one they cut open, they splashed cum into her wounds when she was still conscious, you should-of heard her moan. silt wishes he'd licensed that recording to an 0898 number, make another killing, two birds for the price of etcetera.

he replays the sounds at night, gets him off quicker than counting sheep. silt finds it hard on top - but on top of the property pile silt is. he houses them all – the princes whores; politicos sons and daughters; future leaders of the free-world; fallen-stars - aye, he houses them all. you want housing in this oozing-city? come see silt, he rises like the cream, or some other substance. his main office has the finest potted-plants, the most chill water-

molotovs happy hour

cooler, assistants in the shortest of skirts, the tightest of tights, the leggiest of legs. his photocopier does 25 pages a minute, colour. as for his property list its no lacking substance - houses, flats, mansions, townhouses, terraces, farmhouses with period features, exclusive new developments, maisonettes, luxury studios. he has a separate office – a different, more discrete phone number for the multiple occupancies - boxes really. but how they fill with students, the low-waged, the unskilled. he likes skimming the councils b&b deals - he's always open for the latest eastern load – whether that be east-oxenforde, eastern europe, or far east.

 a key is a key, a door is a door, and a cunt is always a cunt - but they've got their own wash-basin, share the showers - only fifteen to a floor. he's not a charity - he's got bottom lines, he's got beef and beefeater considerations; silts first class. sometimes when he's got a new buy to rent he goes in with his shiny keys, whips his old soldier out and masturbates all over the shiny floor. so that whatever flooring gets put down - under it all, a patch of white, his.

 in your dreams, silt, in your dreams. truth is it was a once-off load of vietnam-easies. a favour. they were real pissed over the one he dumped. cost him heavy. in reality, he don't have those contacts, the true mister bigs are always watching, seeing how those lower down the chain do business, and whether to buy into their operation. watching the backrooms and the chatrooms. working out if this is their man. scanning his dress code, his car, his bank-account, calculating whether they like what they see. will they make him a player? they set silt a test. gave him a load – said if he could shift them, show a clean head, clean heels, and a clear margin – they'd set him up good. what goes around comes around, and what comes around, gets around. they met him down the line, not amused. but they knew how to secure his silence. something forensics might-of overlooked. so not again, not again.

 silts still topping the estate-agents south-east (excluding london) league, for the fifth year in a row. oxenforde does a different type of exploitation. mostly hiring those easterners as domestics, as assistants, nannies, as hired

molotovs happy hour

help. that way they get their labour and get to fuck them for free – droit de seigneur. know your greek. your latin. and your french.

   silt once stood around bonn square for an entire afternoon trying to talk up the androgynous asian lasses. (once he'd figured out who were the lasses and who were the lads. long hair, tats above the elbows, and indistinguishable nipples all – how hard can it be?). they brushed him aside. pretended he was asking for directions. pity. they would-of got rich too. aint that what they came here for - the cities paved with gold, a veritable eldorado.

   university biotechs working on patenting the genes for four-leaf clover silt thinks. silt dreams up a towerblock of silt, property-pimp he. a power tower full of his favourite girls - those from unimaginable spice-lands - where even the estuary mud is fragrant – they are his favourites. mouths shut - yes, legs wide, school-kilts lifted.

   that's another difference between silt and candide. silt hates anything oral - so wet, unnatural, cold. god, no. candide on the other hand loves to give, receive head. candide also loves kilt. the rough tweedy eroticism of 'em on your legs. candide puts it down to the coldlands enlightenment, such an ancient alliance.

   candide has a recurring fantasy. he fantasises getting a people carrier - tinted glass - real muddy licence plates - so dirty they cannot be read - a driver and three others - and pulling up outside silts and pulling on balaclavas, and hauling silt and his assistants out, driving them up to shotover woods, and holding gun to their heads - and telling them

   - this is your life: this is what you do - fucking folks over; destroying them; shooting 'em up; tearing them apart

   and when they cry and cough, piss theirselves and gag – only then will he ask

   - you do understand don't you - you really do understand

   and when they finally get it, nodding their heads like there's no tomorrow, tears showing they truly do get it then candide pulls back trigger - crack - before letting them go. no bullets, of-course - that'd be cruel. but

molotovs happy hour

candide reckons if they've shat themselves that way, well and truly sprayed the brown then there's no way they can go back to their old ways - not once they've been warned. a recurring dream aye. one day. one day.

   candide tells molotov and bootgirl this out loud, too loud when there's a group of architects in – least they look like architects, no collars on their shirts and severe scandinavian spectacles. they don't order desserts. don't even finish the course they've ordered. candide out too loud in front of 'em on how he'd abduct estate agents - about holding them to it, really holding them to it - making them piss and shit in their thin pinstripes. molotov smiles. it is not a pretty sight though it does keep the mosquitoes at bay. until at last he asks

   - but what if this scare tactic don't work? what if they go back to their selling ways. what then?

   candide hasn't thought on that. but he will. he will.

   bootgirl works for molotov these days. helping molotov out in his wee kitchen is the best. together they've cut and scraped, and carried and scoured, and scrubbed and chopped. they've prepped everything from aubergines to cauliflowers, courgettes to okra. they've kept leftovers for their midnight feasts. molotov microwaving spinach into the perfect red pepper half - knob of butter, grind of pepper. and how to make best use of a rough bulgarian or portuguese red - and its no what you're thinking. there's a competition on how to treat the food of arseholes. and she can keep her eye on candide, his half-mind, half-minded ways. kitchen-portering, prepping and scrubbing - bootgirls fine about it, mol treats her well.

   bootgirl still wants to know why ash keeps that long trench coat on all the time. candides not making any sense - as per usual - all he says is that ash doesn't like showing his wings. candide and ash are also good friends of molotovs, they've also offered to help however they could, but mol dismissed them, his eyes ablaze, saying these were firefights he could manage on his own. having them around, drink his brew, and helping casual was enough. and all the after-hours fun. the camaraderie. mol described them as brothers/sisters in arms – it made bootgirl flush with pride, her tiny

molotovs happy hour

blue nose-stud catching the light.

  best of all they imagined a giant picnic holding up cowl road. all nations represented, thousands of folks eating, sharing, bringing their own fare, swapping, tasting. dahl and samosas and okra and fried spinach and normandy bake and horse-radish and pickled plums and red beans and rice and cucumber soup and noodles and pickled pumpkin and imam baldi and greek dips and fat green olives and hedgerow compote and apple strudel and baklava and galicia melons and ... a carnival of taste, a riot of flavour. all nations represented. they imagined being able to stop the flow of traffic, to stop the flow of property, to stop the flow of mis / distrust, a culinary swapshop, a tablecloth the length of cowl road from the plain to between towns road, a car-free zone, all the schoolchildren turning out in their best carnival mayhem, all the young people doing their best world turned upside down, everyone else doing whatever they please as lords/ladies of misrule – drumming, dancing, cooking, partying, eating, eating, eating – this would put the commune back into community, this would be something folks would still be talking about decades after silt had gone bankrupt, this is true inheritance, something their childrens children would be told, the day we ate cowl road.

  molotovs eyes sparkle as they talk up the grand picnic – he offered to talk to the other cafés, restaurants, foodshops – see if something could be pulled together. but bootgirls growing larger and finding it hard to keep life together, planning for two now, candide has always found it hard to keep anything together, and ash – ash: he keeps talking about taking flight, flying outta here. says he's all but ready. knows he don't belong – though none of them do – but he feels a pull irresistible, wings at his back. ash wants to soar and find that place, that special place – the interstices, the co-ordinates, the route and map though not route-map or road-map, that sense of place, of belonging – something for which he longs. molotov knows one day, in one place, or another, a giant fuck-off slow-food picnic will be had and one that stops the traffic. this will happen, will be held, it is a matter of when and where not if. if not oxenforde, then some other

molotovs happy hour

place.

   mol can brew coffee here or in the next town, all he wants is to get those regular parcels of coffee beans from nicaragua and roast and brew and serve his heady coffees. now the seed has been planted he believes the picnic will take place, and candide / bootgirl and the new one will be there, ash he's got an eye on, he's got an idea of, something he saw back in nicaragua … but those others, he knows even if its a while down the line, some place will stand still, come-together, eat.

   down in bonn square and these fascists out selling papers – or trying to - they're getting hassle - they're no succeeding - say one thing for the folks of oxenforde - they don't buy from nazis; or elect them; not many other towns turn their backs. anyways those paper sales aint going well. ash takes out the lighter he always carries although he don't smoke. as he walks up and into them you hear everyone's voices drop, then stop: like someone has hit pause and itching to rewind and

   - you ever watched fascist paper burn?

   its the cheapest kind - burns at a lower temperature, so ash says. and ash, he takes the fascist paper, their fascist paper, burns it to ash, holding onto it, smearing the off-white into his moth-fuelled skin, rolls up sleeves, rubs it into his neck, face, arms, hands and then, only then does he turn back. the moth-juice still flows across and underneath his skin – a seam, rich and defiant as any deep mine. ash tells them to get back in their van. they don't need telling twice, but race round to pembroke street, jump in the knackered white transit and hit the ignition. only this terrible gnashing, roaring, they've been clamped. fines more than the vans worth. they ditch their losses, head for station, realising oxenfordes streets are not – for them anyways – paved with gold.

   ash is thinking, thinking its like they're all wanting some savage thing, some kind-of uneducated black thing, some kind-of primitive violence. voltaire wrote on it enough. oh aye, ash has read his dictionnaire, his philosophique - specially the bit on kissing; and oral sex - cunnilingus, fellatio, giving head, blow-jobs, mouth to fleshy membranes … point is

molotovs happy hour

voltaire may have been three hundred years ago - but he sure liked his blacks un-tame. oh there be plenty wanting still to be dry-humped by some monster of a noble savage such as ash. the cry of surprise still-born on lips even as their arse bleeds. noble? size-queens with an impossible longing is all ash sees. saddened by how in this country – even among the righteous (especially among them?) - he's become reduced to his member, all those impossible inches. ash knows this aint his place, this is not his country, hooking up with candide has been fun, and he owes him for sure – but he longs, longs for his place in the sun.

ash has dreams of ripening lemons. he imagines what it must be like to have your own lemon or orange tree or coffee bush or somesuch outside your door. a place where you are accepted, one hundred percent, for what you are. no questions asked, none. when he closes his eyes he sees sun broken, refracted, as through water. or possibly leaves. he hears the pull of birds, of wings, of ... of moon and stars and tide. how he longs to navigate. how he longs to be pulled over thousands of miles like swallows or geese or arctic tern. he wants that great surge, that uplift, he feels so strong, light these days – he knows it is only time before he soars, and then from his great height, his great quest, thousands of miles, quartering the globe, and as birds do – finding that spot, that place, that location, hitting on the one place to rest, to be. its coming - this, ash knows. this is what is coursing his blood. his veins. his back is itching, he can feel wings pulling at his shoulder-blades, his great ache for release.

candide knows boundary brook somehow marks out two territories. on the southside he is safe. for now. outside of the boundary brook divide - its too strenuous, too twenty-first century. within boundary brook he recognises workers, labourers, artisans. but somehow a third territory remains teasingly, tantalisingly just beyond. that third territory is a landscape candide knows so well, a place where he expects to walk out and onto moorland - out the city, out - walk out to where peregrine is more than the name of your spouse. candide fully expects to hit the moor, and a far-off brilliance of sea - yet all he finds are condom fish, barbie boats,

molotovs happy hour

crow umbrellas, hops that have escaped the e.u., the bones and barbecues of trolleys taken from supermarkets. sometimes candide rounds the useable trolleys up and sells them back to the supermarkets. with the cash he spends an afternoon buying rounds of coffees at molotovs. he wants to talk about this other place, this moorland alter-ego, where twisted gorse roams free, and adders hiss from deep within. sometimes the gorse is ablaze, and not just with flowers, but a-burning. burning bushes literally. he loves to watch them burn, to twist and smoke so imperially and imperiously, he loves his hair and his periwig scented with burnt gorse. how he longs to tell of this in molotovs, but most of all to share his rare good fortune, buying rounds when he's collected that much cash from off the supermarket trolleys.

trouble is candide sees the north-side creeping. he knows that east oxenforde is being renamed, rebuilt, brandscaped. east oxenforders are so geographically challenged, ask them to pin a tail on a donkey and they couldn't if their lives depended – though they could doubtless tell you what donkey was in latin, and how they arrived at the cross on their backs - allegedly. candide sees his rosemund as a fragile eldorado, he sees east oxenforde is being reclaimed - sees the developers moving in - knows this means – soon enough – he, they - will have to move, move on. near-enough time to move on aye, but last orders haven't been called quite yet.

candide re-enters his estate; there is no ha-ha here. most of the time his world is fogged completely, gone from his mind as cat-food from the bowl, with only a crust lurking days-old near the rim. candide believes he's lasted this long cos he leaves a light footprint. three hundred years strong. on the mumbles sand he believes he will sink in less even than bootgirl. he has promised to take her west, someday. they have printed books there since the seventeen hundreds so they are contemporaneous with him. he looks forward to treading lightly on western sands. look a feather has more impact. or a fever. a fever. he gets ready to flee does candide. packs some food in readiness. his favourites a mutha of a brioche - picked it his-self so he did. hollowed out the innards, placed the magnificent honeyed peri-

molotovs happy hour

wig-like structure to his head and hey-ey-ey presto ... but security moving him on, they don't do visual humour, sight gags in the local co-op. around his estate now he finds rabelais rules lined out. voltaire kicks ass - lined out. pataphysics my arse lined out.

    years closing, they've all worked hard for molotov these past days: cleaning, scrubbing, repairing. molotov knows the pressure is increasing. he's a barometer of revolution, of social change. he wants the place to look sweet for the new year. they've taken a crate of sweet madeira plus squeezed grapefruit juice for bootgirl and they've gone and broken into the botanical gardens, and now sitting there under a golden moon draining bottles of this sweet sweet african fortified vine, raising a toast to more molotovs tossed. new years eve? new years day by now. watch the fireworks blasting off and blending with the stars - perfect - above.

    mol clicks in, kicks in, sees an image, a mirror-image, the spit of ash. he's got a photo of it back home. he makes a new years resolution to pass this photograph on. something for ash to file. for future reference. candides suggestion for a new years day resolution is a campaign to accompany the broadsheet of voltairechoruses with tee-shirt slogans - the first will read heterosexuals get off the pavement. three bottles of the sweet sweet madeira and one carton of best squeezed grapefruit juice are raised to the moon, and four bodies slide into one giggle-pulsating warm heap. molotov suggests tee-shirts reading americans get off the pavement for the next installment. this one brings madeira out through their eyes, eyes weep-weeping a sweet if slightly salty nineteen percent proof african wine.

    the world is ghosted. a heavy frost - each of the plants layered with a heavy light; the sky itself is moony and starry - and lying there, lying there – its now two or three a.m.; but layered against cold - layered with warmth - friendship, madeira - the whole visible world is smoothed and soothed - moonlight means bathed in milk, an incomparable welcome and a wordless prayer to a new year. eventually they break out. in silence, walking their separate routes home.

    gardener is in at 8am on new years day. he never tires. after all was it

molotovs happy hour

not voltaire who said we must go tend the garden? and so the gardener does. he tends to ornamental cabbage, iris, beaded iris, iris arranged by chromosome, flaming iris, king iris, solanum crispum, citrus limon. this day - this crisp clear new years day where the bamboo leaves at eight a.m. are smothered in brittle jewels, dripping ice honey and the sun of this new years day is fed translucent through the thin fingered leaves - ice sliding to earth, gardeners feeling good. later, he will pile mounds of crisp, dried bracken into little wicker baskets to place over deep-buried bulbs, keep them burning under the winter soil

molotovs happy hour

civil wars re-fought

all of them mad on the mary chain - candytalking, psychocandy, sidewalking - oh we got sunshine, dancing at the eighties retro-night down zodiac. the mary chain: a ray of chainsaw in a sunlit world. they are well known down the zodiac – bootgirl in her immense d.m.'s which take on a life their own, candide all periwigged and powdered up – though somehow no-one ever laughs, ash - that long black coat and the mothjuice under and over him working wonders under the u.v., and molotov with his infamous hand-dance stripping down assault rifles routine, no-one trespasses when he dances. him – all 6 foot three barefoot, and bootgirl all five foot nothing booted, they fit when dancing – its kind-of negative space. each occupies where the other doesn't, carving, shaping, sculpting air into something tangible, something graspable, something definable. something with as much blade and bludgeon as the chainsaw buzzsaw arc-weld songs of those brothers reid. and ash and candide looking like half-brothers leastways, no-one queries their right to dance as couple, especially not once its understood how they are under molotov and bootgirls fierce protective gaze. no. this is what passes for nightlife in oxenforde - otherwise its mostly horlicks and toast. candide cadged the idea of chocolate bars off john gay in the 1720's so he says. chocolate bars: this was before coffee bars really reached the cutpurse and slut lanes of london. chocolate bars: its where the louche and the dispossessed hung-out, talking dirty, passing on tips, saliva, old-world infections. kiss my syphilitic lips is not a mary chain song though it could so easily be. chocolate bars, why not? candide floats: one day we're gonna tire of tetleys - tea or pints; and this places never gone for coffee, molotov excepted. molotov says he'll offer chocolate on his menu if candide can come up with an authentic enlightenment recipe and they can source it fairtrade. could be fun. maybe they could re-enact café scientifiques, café philosophiques one night a month. perhaps

molotovs happy hour

lewis carroll could play rhythm guitar.

   this eighties night down the zodiac, candides chosen the sixteen eighties of course - periwig, bodice, beauty-spot - just to fuck everyone's mind. he fucks everyone's mind. bus drivers refuse to stop, taxi drivers move on fast, the twenty four hour garage locks its door, all the way down the road the security guards or the big guys out back, stacking, unpacking, surge to doors - check them out, would deny entry ... but the zodiac accepts them unto its dark bosom.

   then on to molotovs for an early breakfast. americano with two sugars for ash, double espresso for candide, and large cappuccinos for bootgirl and mol. voltaire drank sixty a day, no wonder he shook so, and candide wants to live it up a little. plus a clutch of freedom eggs and two trays of vegetarian sausages. sometimes lincolnshire with oregano, sometimes cumberland with cracked pepper, occasionally welsh cheese and leek, the weakest of french grained mustards, and fruit muffins to embed sausage in, all cooked up at molotovs. they serve molotov for once, they know his kitchens well enough by know.

   - gram parsons? kilo parsons more like - amount of white snow he ingested, i'm telling ya

   the friendly worlds of soundman, a mate at zodiac nights where he spins the decks. most-times soundmans a cd dealer from the long end of cowl, wrong end of town, legend in his own etcetera. with soundman you can always find the beat, the beat, refine the beat - dirty three, early lucinda williams, little axe. oh to hang out in pulse – his sonic-shop, his sound-world which features all the best, the choicest cuts - all that, that ... beat, that pulsing, driving, rhythmning beat. from bob marley to albert ayler to emmylou harris to the black keys to sibelius to marais to julia wolfe to neil young to joni mitchell to tinariwen to rokia traoré. soundman, sound, man: he sure is. he supplies molotovs discs. molotov supplies him with brew. topping him up each morning before he opens up pulse. a tall americano with one fairtrade mauritian sugar – no other will do. and soundman spins the latest, the latest sounds, the imports past them. each

molotovs happy hour

sound to him is a picture, a memory, unique, a polaroid, snapshot moment like a cd held alight in sunlight. candide knows the ford-wars psychs would be keen as mustard, english mustard, not american, but fresh ground mustard with a tad, a smidgeon of vinegar, aye, keen as that kind-of, to label soundman but to the molotov crew he is sound. and spinning his stories like a c.d. hung suspended in the east oxenforde breeze, a jewel, a jewel. he refuses to be part of the beaten generation, refuses to be cowed, but like the freethinkers of cowl works his own grooves, and supplies molotov with a different rhythm, a different beat. they are glad to feed him. raise a mug. cheer when he dj's at zodiac, sometimes clearing the floor with one of his obscurer cuts, clearing the floor so they dance, winged and unhinged. and through the haze and noise their eyes and minds meet. they meet.

silt likes bland sounds. rhythm dependable. something you can wank to. most of all he likes the rhythms of building works, not collapsing like einstürzende neubauten. he gets off on the mix of cement, the crunch of gravel, he likes the cries of insecure tenants as they unravel. he likes ratcheting it up, a brick through molotovs window. molotovs been done twice this year. and we're still in january. insurance excesses gone up and they're putting pressure on for molotov to fit shutters. insurers, they can get fifteen percent off the one and a half k it usually costs. molotovs pockets are not that deep. but his fists are stuffed deep into them. some nights he beds down out down there. it's come to this.

ash and candide and bootgirl help out sweeping up the stalagmites and stalactites of broken glass. molotovs unsure, for the first time in a long time. he is feeling insecure. there's a time to fight. and a time to move on out. he's not rooted to this place. he's not anchored. coffee can be drunk in many places. and the rules have changed, the rules have changed. this is not the seventies - not a time of fighting in the streets; this is not the eighties - a time of defending the nicaraguan revolution, while hearing all that is happening back in your old land, riots, bootboys, mass unemployment, falklands; this is not the nineties – this is a grave new world. a grave new world, and molotov don't know where he belongs. only time these

molotovs happy hour

feelings still are being alongside bootgirl. he feels anchored when beside her. but that could be anyplace. he can feel his-self widening inside, he is a delta, no longer a mountain stream. but still his eyes speak - any change, any move, movement, will be on his terms.

silt likes to express his-self if not in bricks&mortar then bricks through windows. and molotovs is on meatmans daily route. how silt wants to bust those weirdos who are holding back his property franchise and his (he hopes) massage parlour. he needs to source the young things to please but surely there's gotta be a way?

there's an open window down on eastchurch and white stripes striking up the band. a carl hiaasen wannabe struggles to find the corruption for his latest novella. you just have to look harder is all; walk a little slower; listen in to the phone-calls and the footfalls; lean into the phone-boxes of corn market round dusk; see which way the handshakes or folds of umbrella fall or where, when and how car headlights of couriers pop up. its in the walk and the stonework. the gentle shirts, the buttons and the unbuttoned, the battered, the buttered and the battened down. cavalier dogs and roundhead curs. this is the english civil war being re-fought but oh so civil. ghost tours from the past. periwigs for ever and ever. its smack and the seven last bleeding words on the cross as re-told in english-bloody-rap by the bleeding poet laureate and his regular motions.

and where is bootgirls child gonna grow? this place is so quiet. but it isn't home. sure there's folks polishing cars, re-roofing, planning drives - but its all so nice, so normal. and candide can't remember selling his soul to this particular devil. this aint where he belongs. or longs. though every time candide reaches the boundary brook of cowl he feels that weight lift from his heart; feels less repressed. its like walking across a microclimate frontier, the temperature shifting by degrees.

there's no oppression by beauty in cowl. perhaps that is it. he longs to see the words of papa-san, ho chi minh his-self, all the way to the city centre as all else creeps out. candide longs for a revolutionary wall of truth-tracts - their message unavoidable, this naming and shaming wall

molotovs happy hour

stretching - stretching the texts out to all. oh how he wants. he wants... tells bootgirl how voltairechoruses is about to roll. they hauled a hand-letter-press all the way to the squat in rosemund. incredible what gets placed on freecycle. they've got a beautiful font. they've got black ink, red paper, good anarchist colours. they've got it almost all set. back to front – the type. they've got the paste and the brushes for fly-posting it. they're ready to spread the word, ol' candides gospel. for my sake take care, bootgirl whispers. holds her oldest friend close.

- remember you're next run-in is gonna get you sectioned my friend. the psychs words. we can't have that.

there's wetness in candides eyes. candide admires bootgirl, admires her struggles, her struggling. wishes he could be better for her. hands over a carrier of mothercare baby-grows he's nicked, passing 'em the outside of the alarms, that wee gap at the entrance as he marched on through. bootgirl is minding molotovs, he said he had urgent business to attend to. candide asks when are mol and her gonna get it on? she goes to kick his arse playfully, but her stomachs no longer quite so flat, and he dodges her toes easily

molotovs happy hour

balaclava'd

- landlord bastards, property bloodletters, on your faces now!

silt lurches forward at the shouted command. already he's reached beneath his desk to hit the panic-button installed throughout the chain month after a spate of dog-shit incidents in summertown, spray-paint in headington, plus some fuckers who should be in school ramming the door with their mountain bikes and driving him nuts. eugenics. that should have been the answer thinks silt and we wouldn't have to deal with such shitheadedness but get a better, a more refined type of client. tie the tubes of the bloody rosemunders, do they think we're made of gold? all that birth on the n.h.s. – just a waste of good tax breaks – i mean. all this goes through silts head as he moves forward having hit the alarms - but nothing rings, and no shutters come down. shit thinks silt, pay cash-in-hand and they stiff you. whats this place coming to?

- you in the muddysuit. get. i'm no jerking round

silt tries to get a good look at the face. but all save those dark eyes are balaclava'd. no help there. silt thought that sales of balaclavas had been banned in the recent clampdown on terrorism. he's going to have to recommend it to albion's national security advisor. perhaps he could take-up the slack in that market, monopolize, become official supplier of balaclavas to the s.a.s?

silt moves forward. he knows how to play the warrior-king. next moment his shins explode as something agonising scrapes down them fast - left then right - he can visualise the blood rushing to broken skin. he flops forward, crashes his nose to the floor, it too starts to bleed. striking out the shins is a basic martial arts move as any molotov knows. now he's got their attention. he ties hands behind their backs with gardening plastic ties, available at any plant-store - the ties have a real good grip, and silt feels the blood engorge, try, fail to surge past this restriction. molotov pulls

molotovs happy hour

a rubbish sack over their heads, gaffers them around the neck, tight enough but with a cushion of air inside. that rip of tape when you're tied and blinded makes them wince. silt thinks this must be the sound of back, sac n crack waxing, the sounds of hell. he can feel his balls withdraw into his body like the wheels on a boeing retracting into the undercarriage. molotov orders them to bump, grind the one in front, orders them up and out. they trip, stumble, fall, manage to get up into some kinda vehicle. its engine now running. they didn't see molotov, his gloved-hands, ripping out the properteers phones. doors left open for the local headbangers to do as they like. that's the sort of creativity the local young offenders like. it might be over the papers by morning, but silts property shop'll be all over the roads within half an hour, tops.

    silt twists his arms but they are tied professionally. what irks him most is when his mobile goes and he cannot reach it. instead, it is taken off him, a window winds down, the rush of traffic outside, the hum of concrete and ... his phone rapidly becoming distant. the fuckers tossed it out? do they not understand the value of such things? with this, and the wrist-ties and ... silt feels his heart-surge, takes a deep breath, only his gob fills with plastic and he promptly passes out. its hot, sweaty inside the plastic sacking. sometimes a corner and they lurch, their faces slip, are pushed into the bags, their breath-suck plastic, they gasp, but try and keep it shallow, guessing whether they'll have enough air or if this is it. try not to mind the sweat in their eyes, try not to feel this mornings clean-on best cotton knickers sticking to all their cracks.

    there's a sharp turn. climbing. slowing. the ground under the wheels changing for sure, gears shift, vehicle slows, starts cracking, crunching. woodland? they are pulled roughly outside. they fall. a dead-cats bounce. the vehicle is some way off the ground. they are pushed to kneeling. something cold, metallic is placed at the head of the first one. he begins to protest

    - jeezus, christ, fuckin

    molotov pushes him with the barrel and he topples over face-first into

molotovs happy hour

a pool his own urine. molotov continues
 - now listen up. this gun...
he strikes metal on metal, they're not to know its two lengths of tubing
 - it will be held to all your heads. any guesses why?
silts p.a. attempts to put her hand up, dislocates her shoulder, as the tie bites, faints from the pain and she too keels over. molotov moves to the third party. silt. places barrel to his head, says
 - why? silt? why? think on. think good.
all silt can think is how to keep control of his bowels. they are twisting their way outta him. molotov helps him, helps them all out:
 - this is your life aint it. this is what you do - fucking folks over; destroying 'em; shooting 'em up; tearing 'em apart in property deals
two bin-bags on the muddy ground nod numbly, the third - silt - still kneeling - shakes from side to side. silts convinced he heard the click of a hammer being pulled back. he's never heard anything so loud. its metal went through his skull-bone like a downturn in the market, no make that a full on market crash. a black-day, yes. the reality of all this shoots through him like a bad tooth. then all goes blank. silts forgotten to breath. reptiles crawling onto land and giving up gills were definitely a retrograde step in silts case. molotov tells the other two there's no second chance. the next-time they will get a bullet. they nod their plastic, agreeing. he tells them to give up property. work somewhere else. or else ... they are already drafting their resignations.
the jeep they were driven in is a cherokee with dark-glass. it carries the plate: silt1. molotov cracks open the fuel tank, takes a quick-suck on a long tube, winces as the gas almost hits, loads his bottle. stuffs his balaclava in as rag. he knows his stuff. lets it catch a while, then hurls it into the vehicle. he retires them all to a safe distance, into a hollow upwind. there's a crackling, a restless energy deep in these shotover woods. flames lick faux-leather, liking what they find. most of all the blue of petrol waiting, then boom and a rush of air in. glass cubes out like frosted sugar. small explosions. paint bubbles. seats pop and crackle. the sputter, splutter of

molotovs happy hour

black smoke, its plastic heavy among the trees and leaf mould. then the gas tank takes, an explosion which leaves the three wrapped figures, all shuddering, shitting, praying. this is the signal for molotov to leave. that fireball will have been spotted. ten minutes and a helicopter'll be over. twenty minutes and the fire-brigade sirens will be heard pulling up the slopes. but molotov is used to deep cover, this operation is his, even in a dead zone they couldn't find him.   the cherokees all but burnt out now, its tyres drooping with heat.

silt is flailing on the ground. molotov, having eased the first twos bindings so they'll be able to claw themselves free in a few minutes of trying, leaves them there on shotover hill. molotov is running silently, leaping over fallen silver birch, until he blends with muntjac deer, with adders, with badgers, woodpecker, magpies. he reckons those properteers learnt the lesson but he will keep his eyes open.

the other two manage to shake the bags off - they don't look back, they thought there was something about silt. they had not put finger to it until now. knowing how close to getting burnt they were, they run through the woods and away. they want to be far off from the burn, the heat, the filth and sweat of plastic. they will shower long but still not get rid of the stench of plastic and piss and sweat that fills their nostrils. their trousers will be thrown out – no ridding them of the memories of writhing in their own cack. it will take some time. truly. they shake. shudder. not looking each other in the eye. just glad to be away from silt. to be away from that creepy woodland. to be away from the burn most of all. to be away from that.

silt nurses his vengeance like a solitary drinker cradling his pint. he remembers where he has heard that exact-same engine sound - every morning - the memory returns as he lies in plastic. if some fucker has torched his cherokee ... he forgets again to breath, falls sideways, lies in plastic. he can hear vague traffic sounds. knows he has to head towards his kind. he stumbles up and off, rolling downhill, getting caught in brambles, which rip the plastic, let some air and light in in. he has got used to this vague light coming through plastic and the slight air. silt can't think

molotovs happy hour

of any enemies. not one. not one with guts leastways. or this much imagineering. silts bag is ripped in places, and he is disorientate. dizzy. he heads towards traffic. knows what he is doing in this at least.

   at last the sound of traffic is loud. but then silt stumbles, bounces, twangs off some wire, can hear its peculiar guitar-struck resonating as he bounces back, falls headfirst. picking his-self up again silt approaches the wire more cautiously this time, finds the wire while probing with his foot. leans gingerly forward to see if there is more, higher. finds one above his groin. he shuffles, bends, snucks through the two strands of wire, the sound of traffic buzzing, feels like he is winning this demented sack-race now he is through the wire and ... foot tangling with some discarded roadside sign, he rolls directly into the path of the oncoming a40, knocking his-self unconscious on the tarmac.

   p.c. hoppers been redirected from patrol. there's a disturbance off the london road. some maniacal evangelical has gone ballistic, doing his nut. he's been this way since the schism over frothing homosexuals in the church. now he's entered the temple, otherwise known as the university publishers, to kick over the tables. only he's had difficulties finding any. instead he is judging those publishers of voltaire whose beliefs are

   - sick secretions of morbid minds,

   he's going over to glossolalia shortly. only in oxenforde the p.c. swears as he floors it.

   p.c. hopper driving, swears again as he sees a bag moving, rolling, it weren't just a rubbish-sack, no, looks like a – a figure? his instinct takes over, he hits the brakes, the rover gracefully being brought under control - but is there distance enough? cop-cars slowing, p.c.'s foot to the floor of the brake, but the bag looks larger each fraction of time. p.c. doesn't have time to feel emotion, but steers into the slight gravel skid, depressing brakes with all his weight, and the precise moment that the car slows and stops is the moment that it touches silt, gentle as pulling a leek from the ground. silt feels some impact. forgets to breath. blacks out again. p.c. hits blue-lights. races to the rubbish-sack. tears out an unconscious silt. p.c.

molotovs happy hour

gags at the stench of piss and shit, vomits unfortunately over silts shirt. silt is breathing and moaning. p.c. radios for an ambulance, takes silts pulse with the least contact possible, tells him not to move, tells him its all going to be ok.

silt feels like shit, moans, nurses his vengeance silent. what really adds insult to injury is spending a night on the n.h.s.. his health insurance is platinum but the private hospital he insists they drive to refuses admission saying they can't deal with possible head injuries, out-of their league, he'll have to go to the ratcliff, sorry, but they could phone ahead, see if he could get a side-ward, how about that? that really is too much.

his story appears in the next days oxenforde mail but short on facts. bootgirl reads it out loud to candide and ash.

- bloody hell candide. what were you thinking? you gotta be careful. you don't want to get caught.

- weren't me. i swear. me and ash were working on voltairechoruses that's all

candide looks sideways to the mirror where molotov observes him with dark, impassive eyes.

the hospital gives silt the all-clear after his overnight, discharge him having issued the standard medical advice to take it easy. silt is reduced to begging the a&e nurses for one pound seventy for his bus fare into the city as his wallet got lost in the cherokee fire. painkillers first then pain is the order of the day silt reckons. silt steps off the number ten bus at the corner of the high, progresses to his bank to sort out new cards. its another bad smack day down on corn market. silt is fucked off by all them bleared-out addicts, propping up the phone-boxes, the benches, and the doorways - he feels nothing for them.

candides saddened by these same addicts, though he knows he can't get involved in feeling sorry for them any more. he watched another best friend die that way - she'd been to hell, never came back - one last, small twisted act of creativity on her part - knowing her life was irrevocably fucked - she spiked it in and slumped away, and candide held her until she

molotovs happy hour

was not. he agreed to be there at the end. this was all she had to look to. she knew she was a goner. knew there was no future. she'd been fucked, fucked over and now all the poor bastard had was to get out the only way she had. and candide understood. he didn't renege. but held on to her, holding on through it all. saw she was cremated so no bastard could claim her resting place.

he scattered her ashes off the broken coast: saints head, the westernlands. she was finally free on the swelling tides off-of those clifftops and islands and inlets. she haunts candides dreams still. its not that he don't care. its that he cares too much. can't anyone else see? candide sees into them as he walks down corn market - can they no see how silt and his bastard-ilk are taking them and hanging them out oh-so-public to dry? candide can't cope with the twenty-first century. feels like he is pulling back the skin, looking into the folds within. raw so raw, yet no-one else sees. when candide walks down streets he can see into peoples very being, he has this gift. he looks within, peers into rib-cages, into viscera, above all into minds, sees the pain, the degradation, the hurt. its not a gift, this vision-thing, its something sent to torture him. he tried explaining it to the c.p.n. who then starts twitching. never a good sign that. and today, this bad-smack-day - it seems so obvious to candide that there's a new deal out, a new strength or dealer or somesuch. whats the word on the street? whats this latest brew called: white-death? ratcatcher? empire strikes back?

its like walking through brueghel or bosch. look at those two over there - crutches are all that keep them above ground - as they perch into the phone-booths; down by the newsagents there's three under cardboard, are they still breathing? even the dogs out-of it. there's one on every cash machine. more on each bench. and those that don't have a perch, hungrily eye the spaces between shoppers. candide can't bear it any more. its like that ache of scarce-knitted bones in the months after another break. in some weathers the pain just will out. candide starts to howl. he gibbers. and rages. he just wants that rage out. he starts to blubber, to shake with despair. pedestrians don't meet his eyes.

molotovs happy hour

candide don't remember making it back to the eastside but he has. he loses time often. sometimes its hours. days. once it was nearer a hundred years. his mind is stilled somewhat by what he has spotted in vixens window: a sublime headpiece - half moulin rouge, half mardi-gras - a periwiggers fantasy in pink featheroons, and he wants, wants bad, wants now - trouble is - it wont fit his swollen head. his head is not on the petite side. instead he is left to dream. and dream he does. its the only thing relieving his pain.

in molotovs he comes up with boas sans frontière - in kingfisher, renegade red, and eye-green. he wants to send them on peacekeeping missions the world over. his other invention is see-through rubbish sacks. who'd want all the neighbours to see your waste from last nights dinners, the clothes you're tired of, the cycling proficiency certificates, old n.h.s. specs – all hoarded for your last decades. who'd want to be known by the rags of last seasons wank-dom. hardcore animals? homeboys and down-boys? anal-mammas – the uniform issue? would you want to be known for this rather than sponsoring next doors kid? all your secrets out. oh yeah see-through rubbish sacks just could be the next big thing if only candide was minister for waste. now it just might be boas sans frontières pipping that at the post. candide wanting to be foreign minister with this idea. candide is so perfectly serious that his friends heads hurt - and they love him, they do – but they ache with trying to follow the rococo of his mind, its curling parameters.

- boas are the answer to world peace. forget blue-berets, send in the boa brigade. gaza, chechnya, nigerian delta, the western sahara even - and all decked in boas. you couldn't fight that. get them adopted the   world over - could have a warehouse in the leys that parachutes them into troublespots, wrap one on around and hey presto no more war. everyone laying down their weaponry in wonder, a kind of olympics of style. if they need grievance they can just award points on length and swish and style and substance of their boa, receive a huge silver cup for their efforts. war no more.

molotovs happy hour

bootgirl laughs. she's deputising at molotovs. molotov likes her a lot. he just can't get the words out right. he knows she's running to the bogs, puking. he's watched her wee skinniness fill out, jeans stretching, button straining, and now undone. he's offered her a regular shift, taking her under his wing, his heart soft as fuck, unlike his fists. molotov has his regulars. he sees they're alright. its the irregulars who are the problem. and today this daft-twat in a lord of the manors tweed flat cap is ordering in the american fashion

- that's a tall low mocha and lightly whisked

bootgirl gets level with the eyes under that turd-coloured tweedy-hat - she's itching for her steel toe-caps to connect with his crotch

- sir we do espresso, we do cappuccino, i do ristretto for my lovers. we don't do subservience. now d'ya want that piping hot to your shrivelled white parsnip of a crotch or d'ya wanna get?

and she escorts him to the door with

- get outta east oxenforde, get back to your estate agents, your p r o p - erty managers, your letting services ... and your flaccid english vegetables.

she goes to polish the knobs on the gaggia. candide winks and grins. his reflection in the polished steel is horrifying.

bootgirl turns her attention to ristretto and restraints. she's the one mothers warn their daughters about. and do they listen? do they fuck. but that's cool cos each generation defines its own footwear - this ones stitched and d.m. bootgirls a tango of the moon at one a.m or pouring salsa through driving rain, orbiting at a midnight service station and laughing her head off.

what d'ya say to someone who asks you to wear boots? this is her koan; her meditation; her questioning. though sometimes the answer arrives too late. and most times the question is asked too late. and sometimes it isn't a question, and night-times, alright times, those nearly-believing it if you mostly close your eyes and whisper, whisper, whisper - she dreams: dreams perfect metallic grape-colored d.m.'s, that perfect boot, a perfect fit, because, just because ... she is bootgirl; and she is cool; and still she don't know. candide with all his wisdom, or folly, of his 300 years, holds bootgirl close, smothers her with his arms, so he doesn't have to look within, witness her pain. bootgirl whispers in candides ear

  - still taking your meds?

  yes though they make him feel like shit.

  official side-effects are rashes, swollen tongues, swollen joints, dizziness, high temperature, rigidity, confusion, agitation, sweating, jerking, hypomania, bruising, bleeding, flushing, fainting, unusual heartbeats, constipation, diarrhoea, sickness, weightloss, weightgain, grinding teeth, spasms, yellow skin, difficulty urinating, loss of balance, slurring, trembling, pins and needles, burning or sensitive or hypersensitive skin, hypomania again – just to be on the safe side – don't want suing, impotence, menstrual disturbance, loss of breast milk, sweating, tinnitus, low blood pressure, lowered platelets, reduced kidney functions, reduced liver functions, rarely death. candide wants to tell bootie how much he loves her but he can't. he blames it on the meds even though tonguelessness isn't on that official list.

  she asks him if he can mind the bar as she needs to go piss. the babbys weighing on her, just like its weighing on them all, even though they don't say. mind the bar? candide doesn't mind. bootgirl returns.

  and then ash turns up. with two carrier bags. one contains paste and a brush. the first edition of voltairechoruses they'd printed earlier but candide had forgot to carry on in. a broadsheet in the anarchy colors – its black type on red. the first fistful of its number are spread around molotovs. then candide and ash hit the backways and byeways, the roadsides and not-so-highways, they hit the council approved flypost sites, and those unapproved. its posted-up, pasted up. across hoardings. its in phone-boxes for all to access. its on community noticeboards, on wholefood shop noticeboards, in pulse the record shop and cyclo-analysts the bike shop; voltairechoruses is making inroads. its telling the story of the estate-agent seized as a lesson to all and offering a different interpretation to that car-

molotovs happy hour

ried in the oxenforde mail. it doesn't condone the act but does say its inevitable if the uncivil attacks on the right to be housed continue in this inhuman way. it tells of shameful rates of multi-occupancies, it tells of the shameful price of peppers (seventy five pence each!), it tells of punishment beatings by psychiatric nurses, it details response times to 999 calls in the unposh parts of the city, it tells of arms deals, property speculation, royal spending. it provides bad bad jokes

- what do kermit the frog and alexander the great have in common? their middle name.

it tells how to claim free personal alarms and where to seek advice on mental health, on housing, on printmaking, on composting. voltairechoruses wants to name names, shame them: the wife beaters, property cheaters, repealers of dream. broadsheets on counters and flypostings at the bus-stops. voltaire has arisen from the dead and is candidly campaigning against property abuse. silt is desperate to find out whowherewhy, to return fire, to do the dirty, to escalate the war.

molotov knows things are moving fast. he takes ash aside, gives him this photograph of a northern nicaraguan mural, this figure with wings, surrounded by the folks of the village, all happily together, mol tells him to add it to his collection. molotov knows why ash keeps his coat on. he's heard 'em say often enough: to cover his wings. molotov imagines asking

- may i touch your wings.

then

- wow. beautiful man

molotov knows his hands are capable of being soft, so soft. knows how it is to be so believing. he imagines ash must be able to feel his wingtips quivering. but he fears somehow his touch would not be light enough – that's what molotov fears most, that his touch is still too rough. so instead he touches ash gently on the shoulder, holds his eyes, holds the gaze, says

- i believe in you.

molotov cracks a roasted coffee-bean between his stained teeth – that's what they used to do in the old sandinista days. chew on coffee beans to

molotovs happy hour

keep them awake and ready through the firefights. when reagans army of terror was close they'd suck on the beans instead, in case the crack gave away their positions. molotov grins at ash, folds ashes hands around a worn photo of this mural he came across. a figure, like ash, strong-built yet lean and winged. molotov adds

- i believe in you. know you'll post the photo back someday, let us know you're safe. but for now, keep it safe.

molotov folds ashes knuckles around this photo, and holds him tight. next molotov hands over this well-worn map, a wee circle in purple on this place in the north of the country. mol holds ash tight. the image is strong, and ash recognises his-self, its real in him, and above all he feels that impulse to soar, and fly

molotovs happy hour

grave new world

- you realise most garages taped up with heavy plastic and used late at night are either bomb or drug factories?

thus started a late night conversation over the phone. someone in rosemund half-jokingly, but only half, talking about the queer comings and goings from the garage on that patch of land nearby.

- two weirdos – perhaps harmless – but one never can tell. long leather trench coat, black as he is, though you know i'm color-blind really i am. and this other one, spends his time dressed like the b.b.c. on a sunday evening - jane austen or dickens

and it all escalates from there.

ash tries cheering candide up but candide is so bloody tired. all he can think is three hundred years, three hundred sodding years without rest, without sleep, without home. moving, moving on, its not crows-feet around his eyes anymore, its ravens-feet, bloody huge ones at that. candide just wants rest. he's even given up wanking, this is how tired he is.

they are suddenly aware of noises outside, a mixture of low, slow footfall, then an unnatural hush. clicks, whispers. then a low-moaning buzzing buzz-sawing, chain-saw, closing in, ashes worst fears - helicopter blades. and then the bright-light of god as all hell descends, flashlights on full, searchlights on max, you are surrounded, door down, ash only just has time to look at his joint, drugs dog takes one look at him, rolls over plays dead - their handler not best pleased. then a stun-grenade hurls smoke and confusion. the grenade has taken ash out cold. what candide see is this. this team in bug-eyed sunglasses though it is night, entering like liquid mud. they're wearing sandy brown outfits, thick kevlar, guns strapped left to right. ammo belts, walkie-talkies, confusion, ash out for the count - a swelling on his left temple where they scored a direct hit. candide looking up, nothing surprises him anymore, he is that tired.

molotovs happy hour

- weapons inspectors? you wont find anything here. try the railway station, left luggage. or the arms and business school next door. perhaps r.a.f. brize norton?

they don't even tell him to shut-it, just stand on both wrists, another places a size eleven desert boot on his throat, forcing him down to darkness. he is a soft blanket collapsing, folding in on itself, again, again and again.

when he awakes next, ash is gone.

- wheres ash?

they give blank-faced stare. eight pairs of insect eyes try to bug him out. the helicopter blades are receding but the light is still intense, immense. there is a chatter of communications, the occasional burst of static, the only thing that gets reaction is

- brown-shirts were outlawed as a form of allegiance in this country after oswald mosley you know

american voice from somewhere outside his sightlines gives an order

- shut the goddamn fuck up

another of the bug-eyes leans forward, candide feels something scritch-scratching his arm then ...

candide dreams. all form dissolving. and so vivid. he loses his identity submerged in this hallucinatory liquidshift of nothing and everything morphing, faces leering, and places he's never been, yet familiar, so familiar, like archaeology, like scraping back the layers of history – here a tudor layer, there a viking, there – stone age. finding buckles and boots, pottery, tools, discarded glass, religion, texts, weapons, boats, like archaeologies ... candides mind scraped, layer by layer, unlocking, uncovering the grim, the grime, the grimiest. digging down through the mire, the moorland, the peatbog. the sadness, the insecurities, the memories and the remembrances, the flights, the fancies, the fears. with sodium pentothal, the truth drug, they read his book. they reveal the workings within the workings, the memorandum, the erratum, the footnotes, headers, research-notes, illegible bloody handwriting, backward handwriting, sloped handwriting,

molotovs happy hour

brushstrokes, calligraphy, scratchings on stone and slate, they peel him layer by layer. they want his workings, his ghost in the machine.

all the joint-task force, the anti-terror team, find is – strange fruit, strange strained fruit, ramblings of psychosis, death of a beloved, scars, scares then suicide attempts. and some chemical stew, some nightmarish brew poisoning candides mind, legacy of some long departed beloved he has left behind. volt. was that the name? someone dead, buried but not in his mind. this volt runs through, coursing, current. they don't find terrorism. they don't find drugs baron. all they find is an unhappy, fucked, scrambled mind. and all they find in the garage is bare lives. a joint is the only actionable item. though a camping gaz stove is sent off for analysis just in case. they uncover nothing more than bedding, blankets, duvets and carpeting stolen from skips; a few paperbacks: voltaire - candide, hesse - steppenwolf, kafka - the bucket rider and other writings, the cyborg handbook, chaosophy, angela carter fairytales, an old fashioned dictionary in french, poets of the revolution and ashes postcard collection. his postcards of cherubim, seraphim, angel of the north, angels of the south, sheila na gig, cromlechs, outsider art, sunsets and eclipses. and ash? disappeared. gone. ashes to ashes, dust to dust. he is off the records. written-out. an unperson. not a trace remains. not even his long leather jacket. every trace of ash, in the wind, gone. dust to dust, ashes to ashes ...

there's also a knackered old portable cd player plus a single speaker. and beside it c.d.'s from soundman - ayler, mingus, oysterband, penguin café orchestra, jo-ann kelly, nina simone, blind boys of alabama, mc5, townes van zandt, saariaho, strozzi, monteverdi –they some kind-of poof? the commander mutters. batteries used and unused, a packet of peruvian fairtrade coffee – which provokes most scorn, a billycan, packets of noodles, a bread knife and a letter press for hand-printing – still lettered from voltairechoruses, scene-of-crimes are in disturbing the typesetting – they think it may-of been satanic at first with its words all back to front; takes them a while to work why that is, then they realise. oh.

so voltairechoruses is down after one edition, like so much else this life,

molotovs happy hour

the printing-press impounded for further tests. candide sent from reinforced police-cells when they realise there's no terror, no terrorism, only possession of a joint they can charge him with. shit – they thought they'd scored big time. there's a new pay-deal in on performance related pay, but no they hadn't scored a class one terrorismo, they've lost their bonuses, and once they lose those they lose interest real-quick. and candide? he's returned to the ford-wars, lorazepamed and pinioned for the journey then placed on heavy-duty antipsychotics, so heavy-duty there's a string of spit at least a foot and a half long hanging out side his mouth. his bed in i.c.u. has been specially prepared, next to the nursing station, he is folded into it where he burbles burbles burbles about ash, about ash being disappeared and everyone meets his questionings with blankness

- there's no ash, no fire, you're raving man, raving

the psych-nurses all say and administer higher doses of haloperidol, amisulpiride, largactyl. candide can scarcely recognise his-self these days, spends hours pulling his-self together, lying there in the bed each morning, trying to remember which century he's in and what is his name?

ash has disappeared. and though no-one whispers ashes to ashes, dust to dust, he is off the records, written-out, an unperson, not a trace remaining. except in minds of bootgirl waiting, molotov biding his time, and candide? candide tries keeping the memory of ash strong through psychiatric nights and days dazed

molotovs happy hour

gunpowder plots

oxenforde don't exist. those marks on map are not there. what does exist is a series of villages of the mind. a mental oxenforde. tourists asking where is the university? don't realise the sheer metaphysicalness of this – there are dozens of old-old buildings with names like college this, college that. follow the chinos of the accent-less and you end up ducking through a salmon-stone archway, catching glimpse of some other world before a man in a top-hat says

- we are closed to visitors today but can i interest you in a mediaeval c.d. of our choir?

when approached for directions by outsiders, the oxenforder inevitably replies, turn left, look out for the poster advertising quartets by candlelight, go round the bend, go further round the bend, right round the bend in fact, keep the poster for shakespeare in the park on your right, take the next exit then left right left right, right right right. can't miss it for gargoyles. the japanese bow. the germans look perplexed. swedes say

- ve love your english humour. terry wogan, tony blair, david beckham and flash a v for victory sign. the americans go

- gee, so much hisss-tory. is there a crapper? d'ya have a teashop. d'ya gift-wrap?

oxenforde aint the only thing not to exist. ash has flown the coop, disappeared, gone. no trace remains. candides mind-blown, wandering, alone.

when molotov and bootgirl attend the main cop shop down saint alldates, beside the river, a river everyone else knows as thames and this oozing-ford place knows as isis, they find this desk-sergeant, a right porker, someone who knows how to make a bacon sarnie weep. he looks them up and down, looks down, keeps chewing. if he keeps chewing his brain works, approximately. he daren't stop, or it will all seize up. his head aches.

molotovs happy hour

his jaw aches. he's terrified of the dentists chair, what happens then? what happens when they ask him to take the wrigleys outta his gob, stop chewing, open wide, what then? he will seize up. he daren't take this to thames valleys occupational therapy, he knows what they are thinking, their voices buzz in his skull. so much noise, like all the calls on his radio, filtering them out, keep chewing, keep on keeping on, head down, jaw-jaw. he hasn't heard of the new 'citizens charter' for the police, isn't interested in thames valleys customer satisfaction surveys, their charter marks, quality assurance programmes, plain english campaigns, their consumer -facing policy, its all he can do to keep his jaw moving, he can't sleep, and fillings rattle his skull. shortly he will do a runner, leap off folly bridge, and drift, magnificent and manatee-like down the thames, all the tourists flocking and filming, marvelling at his spouting water. this is the place that gave us alice in wonderland you know – they nod their heads wisely, check the time. he will end up beached on a small island before iffley lock, the firebrigade hoisting him out as they would any stranded cattle, and then he will end his days, happily grazing, chewing the cud in the ford-wars psychiatric hospital, believing he is the lead heifer in a prize-winning herd of jerseys, and he? - he gives the best gold-top. burn-out is the jargon. a place in panto beckons but he is too busy chewing, chewing. let someone else worry about global warming, about low-methane cud. his udders ache. he needs to chew.

molotov, bootgirl try and keep their cool. they wait. five minutes in they ring his bell again. his head remains down, only his eyes move - yeees?

they start to ask about the raid, ashes disappearance, candides imprisonment in the ford-wars psychiatric hospital. the raid has been in the oxenforde mail, its been on community tele channel six, the local mp made a statesmanlike statement about how

- with all the terror around these days you can't be too careful at all

before returning to his red boxes, his chauffeur driven car, being driven away. copper chewing cud doesn't answer their questions, he rings the bell his-self and soon a bright young thing, a fast-tracked, fresh-faced recruit

molotovs happy hour

with a 2.1 in psychology and a brown-nose from police college whizzes through, smiles pleasantly and offers to take them through to an interview suite. in the corner is a potted plant. it contains a small cctv, a mike and a spurter of cs (gas not lewis) to subdue any 'unexpected' acts of public. the plant is near-dead. whiz-kid offers tea, coffee. they decline. then she calls up a press officer who comes through with the relevant info. turns to them saying
   - your relationship with mr er, um, candide. did you say you were his sister and brother?
   family, yeah, molotov nods his head. knowing from past experience they wont release info to 'friends' and he can't be arsed getting into precisely what shape this family tree takes – not pear or damson or medlar for sure.
   - well, um .. its down to the c.p.s. of course but we think this one should just be quietened up, you know? in his best interests. not been well has he for some time?
   about 300 years whispers bootgirl. molotov nudges her. he is icily polite when dealing with the police. he's used to seeing the whites of the enemies eyes out there in the nicaraguan cloudforest between lago de apands and nuevo segovia.
   - so you think the mental, er, psych hospital where candide is will be the focus for his future and not the law?
   - oh yes, i should think so
   molotov and bootgirl exchange relieved glances. so he's to remain locked up for a while. its not the first time. wait for those meds to kick in, wait for them to take effect, his thoughts quietening, if only they can get him to keep his mouth shut until he is outside, they'll look after him on section 117 release, the periods of relief from hospital getting longer and longer, until a care plan review, the section lifted and they can all move on.
   - now for ash.
   - ash: i'm sorry?

molotovs happy hour

   - yeah ash. big guy. six foot, black, long trench coat, wings. can't miss him
   - now look. if this is some kind-of prank. wasting police time is an offence you know
   bootgirl kicks in
   - no time wasting. he was with candide. what mol my brother here
   she gives him a big brotherly squeeze on his arm to add emphasis
   - was saying. ash. tall guy. long coat. he likes to wear party-wings. one of his things
   press-woman consults her file
   - no. sorry. no-one else present. candide was alone. all alone. i have it here in writing. can show you if you like
   molotov clenches fists. bootgirl gives molotov another reassuring squeeze.
   - now if there's nothing else
   press-woman rises, makes gesture toward the door and holds out her hand, the psy-ops brown-nose does likewise. molotov and bootgirl rise. molotov looks them in the eyes without blinking. he keeps on staring until their eyes water up, they blink, look away. there's a cover up in force but why?
   the desk sergeant keeps chewing, keeps on chewing, god - his head hurts and how, he gotta keep on chewing. psychological-operations and press-woman close the door. exchange glances. psy-ops says
   - now that went well. didn't it. i mean. all things considered
   press-woman mops her sweat, shakes the blouse out from her drenched under-arms, reapplies her smile and makes for the locker room where she will also reapply deodorant, a big splurge that will leave the next shift gagging.
   molotov shaking his head, bootgirl takes his arm. he knows he should get back, open up but ... he has to blow-off steam. they cut through church meadows, come out by the botanic gardens. molotov strides across the road, a hulking cherokee jeep oncoming. molotov turns. stares. don't

molotovs happy hour

move. driver hits the brakes. molotov stares it down. stares it down. puts his hands on the bonnet. then lunges for the windscreen. and bellows. lets out all his pain. his rage. his frustrations. his ... his punch is enough to crack the glass. sure enough a thin spiders-web of fissure spreads through the safety glass of silts new cherokee.

    driver silt catches a last glimpse of molotovs eyes through this crazy-paving. swears he's seen 'em somewhere before. remembers he has from beneath a balaclava. then cacks his-self. silts bowels just turned to peatbog. he empties his-self all over the upholstery. and his jeep only five days old. his new bloody cherokee. someones gonna have hell of a cleaning job and even then there will be a stain. and all after his previous cherokee torched. silt subconsciously knows this, he sees the stain, tots up columns of figures in his head, works out whether he can afford to trade it in already. gotta get cowl road up and running first he realises. the new branch office. sub-lets above. buy to rents still rising nicely thank you mammon. and office space. and a few extras, the vietnam-easies. get meatman and his nazi others to put the hurt on that fucker in-between times. and how come that fuckers there in front of him now. and how come he's got same eyes as the fucker who made him shit his-self just those few days before. oh fuck. oh. fuck. oh

    silt will now work to get molotov off cowl road. oh yeah. get some real special deal worked out. hit him where it hurts. hit him in the balls. and then the wallet. cowl road. that's where the cash-cow resides. the percentages aren't in risinghurts or rosemund yet – they just aint eldorado. but cowl road and east oxfenforde – now that where the cherokee dealership should be. the horns of cars behind are going crazy. traffic backed up beyond the roundabout at the plain : this awful memorial - some anniversary of queen victoria - the fountain dry as her reign. silt manages to crawl on, his head out the side window, only way he can see, steering for merkin street or merton lane where he can pull in. harness his rage. clean trousers and twenty four hour window replacement. then revenge. tomorrow bright and early the squeeze begins. he can't wait to see the pain, the look

molotovs happy hour

in that fuckers eyes. taking molotovs ball sac and squeezing and squeezing and squeezing. god, it reminds him of sunday school!

bootgirl takes molotovs hand leads him towards south park. they stop at this wonderful lebanese place at the bottom of the hill. molotov - spent, is parked outside like a loyal guard dog. inside bootgirl purchases crispy falafel, thick baklava, apricots, water, leads him into south-park. two thirds the way up the park is the picnic tree, her favourite one. oak. she feeds him falafal then baklava, apricots, fizzy water. they sit, looking out over oxenforde, the reaming spires, the puking accent-less students, the car wars, the gas escaping from balloon flights, civil wars re-enacted just for them. the lines of pikemen, yeomen, shotsmen, dropping to their knees, firing, reloading as the second rank fire over their shoulders. they see the smoke. they can smell the cordite. the gunpowder plots. they witness civil war through the haze.

- what next? where do we go from here? what the fuck is it with ashes disappearance?

molotov turns to bootgirl. bootgirl folds his hands to her stomach, taking his large hands to be warmed, taking him to her warmth, this big man, kindest she has met, this molotov, he's got so much bottle. all she hears is this roaring like b-fifty-two's hurtling down a runway. he gives her a hug, pulls her to feet.

- we got a new delivery in about half an hour – the best jinotegan and matagalpan beans. feral trade. these trade unionists who have come to give a speaking tour brought the coffee beans in their personal luggage. wanna put these beans into roast soon as possible.

they head back to molotovs together. she gave up her place – friend of a friend of a friends – out there on the leys, molotov said she could crash. keep an eye out for each other. safer that way. its molotov sand bootgirls now. she offers him a hand. he asks why her hearts beating so fast. has she blown it? she just wants to know if molotov will be more than brotherly, she aches to find out

estralita

molotov gave bootgirl his room when she moved down from the leys. its towards back of the building, away from the road. its done out as cloud-forest. its full of trees. mist. there's a breeze blowing through. the floor is soft, velvety. she wants to ask if he grew up around maurice sendak. did someone read him the wild things when he was a kid? did he take it to heart? molotovs always saying there's a time and a place. secrets reveal themselves no doubt if they feel they can trust you. maybe its like this in his place. bootgirl feels at peace. she feels secure. it feels right. natural. she can't come to harm. above all she trusts molotov, and she don't want to let him down. third night she was there, she looked out and swears she saw a pair of yellow eyes like lemons watching her. she asked him in the morning.
  - black panther
  - you're kidding
  - naah black panther serious. its a good sign seeing her. they're more afraid of you than you are of them. we are the alpha predator not t h e m . if she's come that close it shows she trusts you.
  and he tops her mug up and offers a second camembert and walnut pancake, one of his specialities. she doesn't know what to make of all this panther talk - is this mols idea of a joke?
  there's a sudden hammering, a drilling, an explosion of plaster, of knocking up of scaffolding before eight.
  - what the?
  bootgirl races through to look out onto cowl road.molotovs wearing his favourite sari – the one with the nicaindios petroglyphs – the original peoples and artworks of his beloved republic, nicaragua. he tightens the sari against his skin, moves to the window beside bootgirl. workmens vans outside. on both sides. mol storms downstairs, barefoot, wrapped only in

molotovs happy hour

sari, nothing else. bootgirl pulls on leggings. her tee-shirt reads hope not hate from philosophy football.com –profits to the anti-fascists at searchlight, that's what she likes to see. comrades in arms, a natural fighting pair, try finding, tackling the foreman, who acts ignorant, saying

- orders from silt. downstairs into property-shop and upstairs to be subdivided and let. buildings gonna take weeks - other side? silts got massage parlour planned. choose which asian you want walking down your spine. he's promised me a ten per cent discount.

molotov sees dust and noise all hours of the day and evening even before the destruction of his wee community these properties are bringing. molotovs is not gonna be a place to sit, drink fairtrade brew, read liberation, wire, fire, neon highway, phosphorous or the latest anarchist studies. they're gonna be draining the electricity, maybe shorting out that side of the street, water pressure'll be way down for weeks

- progress mate. progress. besides

he points a spirit-level at the window of molotovs.

- you could get a good price for selling out ... looking tatty.

bootgirl has to hold molotov back. molotovs like the mustard in a sandwich. he's being squeezed. dangerous signs.

meatman turns up before his meat round to give a hand. silt pulls up too. they look at molotov. sneer. molotov steps closer. meatman points a finger in molotovs face. then a rare flash of genius. with his other hand he reaches down. whips at and off molotovs sari. the sari ripped off. and all stop. all stare. nothing there. there's nothing bleeding there. where his manhood should be, some piss-slit, a triangle of pubes, nothing more. no meat, nothing dangling, he is without sausage. he is a she.

the street, the whole street is frozen, even the bus-stop opposite. molotov – naked, dickless, without his manhood - lunges forward, sinks teeth into meatmans outstretched fingers, clamps down, his teeth grinding through skin, through cartilage and gristle, clamps down between the top joint, harder and harder, keeps teeth firm as meatman sinks to his knees, meatman starts to faint from the pressure and the pain. molotov keeps pressure up. there's a crack, rupture. last thing meatman remembers is a projectile spat in his face. in fact his fingertip. no-one else moves. this freedom fighter, this commandante, this guerilla – he's not a guy, he's a chick. he's a bleeding she.

   there's a flash of some sleek black shadow – huge, an impossible, pantagrulian cat, police taking eyewitness statements after the event will put down the descriptions from meatman and foreman of a big beast, some jaguar likeness – as hysteria, pure hysteria. this shadow, this hulking shadow takes up the bitten-off finger tip, makes off with it, an hors d'oeuvre, takes a swipe at meatmans van, his rear-doors. a vicious predatory paw, the pressure per square inch sufficient to bust locks, more. the lock busts, hunks of smoked meat falling to the road, jamming under tyres. cat takes its teeth to a carcass, then turns and arcs a big spray of piss into the interior, its claws to both nearside tyres which hiss and piss their air, and like the air – this black cat too leaps and disappears. foreman and workers meanwhile doing some laurel and hardy routine with a plank of wood and taking out the front windows of molotovs, only to do the same to their own two properties. thick steaks of glass, fragment, fall to the pavement. the bus-queue opposite are hypnotised. meatmans bleeding in the street, needing hospital to cauterize the wound. molotov picks up his sari and gestures bootgirl back inside.

   she looks at him, whispers

   - helluva cat-flap for that?!

   he smiles. only then does he put the sari on. she knows better than to ask. everything has its time and place.

   right now they have to board up window, make it safe. molotov produces his baseball bat. baseball being nicaraguas national sport, starts thwacking what remains of glass outta the frame, onto the still-puking and shivering meatman in the street. the workmen have pissed off, this aint in their contract. tea is. an ambulance has been summonsed. no doubt police are on their way but because of all the blockage - a bus stalled opposite due to drivers gawping he can't now restart his bus, plus the knackered

molotovs happy hour

meat-van which needs two tyres replacing. then there's the falling scaffolding and the foreman treading through the tiptoes of the broken glass, plus the combination of twenty first century traffic through mediaeval streets – means that ambulance or police wont be through any time soon. and meatmans fingertip has got no chance of re-attachment

    molotov and bootgirl work swift. there's boarding out the back from last time the windows got done in. mols window is soon filled. he knows its gonna be 48 hours before replacement glass can be fitted. bootgirl writes out a neat sign closed for repairs: re-opening shortly. molotov nods his head. they fix a big breakfast. leek and cheese veggie sausages, low sugar beans, fried potatoes, organic mushrooms, beef tomatoes, emmental omelette, toast, butter, marmalade. and the first of the new crop of arabica from the segovias, the mountains beyond esteli, roasted right there at molotovs.

    having eaten their fill he asks refill? she nods. he tops them both up with espresso then pats the old chaise-longue he found outside an antiques shop down north parade. north parade is royalist, so stuff 'em, he carried it off. now he starts to talk.

    - fought my balls off in nicaragua. i fought my balls. off. for real. you seen. well.

    bootgirl squeezes molotovs hand tight.

    - estralita means little star. about the first spanish i learnt. apart from comrade. duck. and whaddya mean there's no frigging toilet paper? the first spanish i learnt. was drinking coffee with a friend and we're discussing where is my home? where do i fit? folks everywhere commenting how you're no from around here - your accents no from here. where you from? i mean originally? but i have no roots as such, i've been all over since those early days in the red republic. and there i was drinking coffee in edgecity and we're talking roots, belonging, and longing and my mind blanking out on geography of this city and me thinking home is, maybe, where i drink coffee. and i drink a lot of coffee. and i say this. and my friend nods. and this is why edgecity of course. edgecity: never seen so many coffee

molotovs happy hour

bars, espresso palaces, felt like i could fit in. but then ... then ... one side edgecity is latte and espresso and cappuccino but the other side the street is literally the poverty and prostitution and syringes and blisterpacks of diazepam crusted in car park mud and crime scene do not enter tape tying up the desolate, the concrete, the neon fragments of a city dark as the coffee of night. and i leave the caff, my mind buzzing, buzzing at the meaning of it all. i'm here drinking coffee, but coffees not from here, not from anywhere i know - and i don't now enough about the stuff. and walking the blade of edgecity back home to me squat and this lass, this lass coming up.
   - you wantin business?

and i'm not. not in that game. its a pissing-it night in edgecity. i'm fuelled, coming out this caff, walking the blade home, and this lass, my own age, in denim jacket and short short skirt, legs like raw meat, and denim basies, she comes up offering business. i mean she's real nice about it. she's not aggressive, not pleading desperate though there must be little enough trade in this chucking-it wet. but she keeps pace with me, walks up the street with me, she walks hundred, two hundred yards, now a quarter of a mile, walking alongside, offering business, telling of all the good things she can do. she's asking if i like anal. do i like it without rubbers? she's telling how she could dress up, be whatever i want her to be, be whatever age i want. tie her up. piss on her. that kind-of. this lass my own age and i don't even know who i am. and now this lass, offering herself, or rather some piece of herself, in exchange for a little cash. and here i am walking the edge, walking the blade, treading the blade, and it comes to me, comes to me then. i will never know where i am, who i am unless i choose one side of the edge, or the other. here i am – walking this road – with the poshest of the posh one side, and the red light underbelly the other and i don't fit one side and i don't belong the other. and its make up your mind time. its time to wake up, make up your mind. you know that old phrase, about wake up and smell the coffee. well ...

   i turns to the lass. invites her back. tell her i don't want her. don't want sex. i don't want to 'just talk'. but i tell her if she wants to come back, dry

molotovs happy hour

out, eat with me, share what booze i've got, the fags dry in my pocket, she's welcome. i wont touch her. wont hurt her. don't want her. don't desire her. i am in so many ways like her, i say. we wear the same denim, we walk the same road, only i've not yet come down on one side of the edge. if she wants to get dry, warm up, get fed, then she's welcome. she hooks her arm through mine. tells how she don't like the whoring. tells she aint no junkie-whore, no heroin-prostitute, she's just out there survival-sexing it, nothing else for her now, and how she's fallen one side of the blade. and her name? estralita. little star. from a latin american catholic family trying to make it over here. they're running a wee restaurant / store. only she falls for a guy and she's 15. and she's not supposed to sneak out to see him. but she does. they hold hands. nuzzle in the dark. teenage stuff. she goes on the pill. does this in secret. no telling. its just in case. just in case. a precaution. better safe than sorry. she's not ready for sex, he's not asking. but she's being real grown up. just in case. just in case. only she's spending more and more time with this lad, he's a month younger than her. and her fathers not liking. maybe he's hurting. maybe its jealousy. maybe its protection for her. he knows men can be bastards. maybe he is one. he's struggling. trying to do the right thing. failing. he's failing. he searches her room. looking for evidence. is she smoking? keeping a diary of her inner-most? has this boyfriend given her drugs? he comes across the pill – the packet part-used. she comes home in time to work in the restaurant. he confronts her. there's a scene. a big, big scene. tables overturned. diners not knowing what to do, how to take it, which way to turn. she grabs her denim jacket, walks out. she's been walking since. its been nearly three years. and she does pretty much anything for a bed for the night, some scran, a bit of warmth. whatever. all this with her arm through mine: she tells me this.

i take her back. she gets under the blankets. i cook up this kind-of risotto, thick swamp thing – whatever i got pretty much. we eat. drink. cry. joke through the night. she points out the morning star, says think on me. think on me. kisses me on the forehead. turns to go. and i know its my turn to go. i walk out. don't look back. i keep walking.

molotovs happy hour

    searching for a little justice, a little honesty. its been a long long road. and in my travelling? i looked out for estralita - the morning star. and it looked out for me. looked after me.
    it followed me through europe. drinking coffee in potsdam where my german friends say but your english coffee is so bad, in thessaloniki, in slubice, in clermont-ferrand, in ljubljana. morning star followed me across north africa. drinking the black brew of marrakesh. i even saw the coffee bushes of ethiopia, there in the highlands to the south, where it was all alleged to have started – some goatherd watching his goats get all frisky chewing on this wee bush with these low hung cherry like things, and the lad investigates, tries eating the rind but its disgusting, so he breaks on through, finds these greenish beans and finds if he chews on 'em he gets more focused, can keep awake. but the taste is foul. sun dries 'em out. so he adds water, adds some sweetness. adds some light. you got yourself the brew. and i found this. and i found myself. oh yeah i found myself. and its all borders, coffee is geography and territory, its breaking the borders, and its solidarity and its collectives but its also non-unionized, multinational, top dollar. its geographies straining, machine straining, and underneath there's earth, there's roots, sun, water, crop, there's life and death. underneath there's soil, there's always soil. i guess that's what started coming out then. and why did fairtrade taste like cack? thank fuck its changed now – but back there, back then!
    and on starbucks cups it practically says if you don't buy from us children will starve, they will remain uneducated, they'll not form part of a future market. and edgecity is the fourth city this land of g.b.h., and this coffee thing, this coffee house things a two edged sword of damocles hanging overhead and coffee is stillness, my blood coursing. and at this same time the white house scandal of arming the contras. of putting weaponry in the hands of a bunch of sadistic rapists and killers and asking 'em to shoot up the future. that's why i had to go to nicaragua. that's why i went and fought. i'd been drinking enough of the bloody stuff. didn't know its history. needed to find myself. found myself in nicaragua, planting then

molotovs happy hour

harvesting the coffee, ended up ak47 in hand defending the revolution. i once helped hold off reagans terrorists for twelve hours until reinforcements came, then bandaged the wounded and cried over the dead – those slain by u.s. hate. oh yeah i fought. fought hard. found my side of the blade. but the people. the people! though they had next to nothing, they would share it with you. singing, guitar'ing, so many kids named estralita. made me weep. one was this wee girl. twelve and orphaned. her mother was a soldier until she got killed. her father was 'disappeared' by the contras. and she was being looked after by other folks. and i ruffled her hair said i would fight for her, for the others. for all the estralitas. i would fight for all the estralitas, all the little stars. and i did. oh, i got blood on my hands plenty. one day we celebrated shooting down an american transporter that was arming the contras. that got coverage. made it to the news. folks couldn't ignore the terrorism america was funding, the brutality and murder, tens of thousands slaughtered in reagan and george bush seniors name. many of 'em were farmers, teachers, medics, just doing their job in the warzone.

oh nicaragua, nicaraguita. part of the american empire since the eighteen hundreds. their sphere of influence. their monroe doctrine. sandino rose up. so he had to be slaughtered. the somozas bankrupted the place, ripped its heart out, americans loved that. finally the f.s.l.n. rose up in revolt. somoza saw the murals on the walls. even america was disgusted by the somozas pocketing aid when earthquake struck and twenty thousand died. so a revolution. a popular revolution! the sandinistas won elections. sixty one percent of the popular vote. and a fair vote too. but reagan couldn't stand that. mined corinto, their only deep water port. even the international law courts fined the states eleven billion dollars but the americans gave the middle finger. so we're one edge of the blade - me and the sandinistas, americans on the other. learning the edge, the edge, learning the edge. how the biggest terroristas were the u.s.a. and they god-damn wanted to keep it this way. a free run, a free reign for their bombing campaigns, only compassion comes down to carefully weighted aid to poor countries and a warning how a democratic sandinista victory would not

molotovs happy hour

be in your best interests.
   well that's the edge i fought for. that's the war i fought to discover myself. to find myself. my place. aye, where i belong is where i drink my coffee. the u.s.a.'s refusal to pay compensation for their campaign of terror which left tens of thousands slaughtered, many more homeless, orphaned, the country gutted, and the continued refusal to sign up to international law - cos the u.s. would be judged criminal yet again. and those working in coffee in nicaragua wont ever taste the actual harvest - too expensive. make do with cheap powdered alternatives. couldn't stand that poverty. fought against it. fought against the quest for an american free trade zone. the trickle up theory. pay little enough to bottom of the pile - then by the time it comes into our hands it'll be huge. and they'll be thankful they got something, anything. an i.o.u.. this is true trickle-up. the low wages, low living, appalling conditions spread across a vast continent, across hundreds of millions of people, so that by the savings of cents - across the board by the time it rises up the pyramid - speed increases, the savings magnify so by the time you reach the top you're rolling in it. i fought back then. now my coffee comes from their collectives, pays a fair wage, puts money back into those same villages where i held a gun, pays for schools, schoolbooks, a health-centre, a communal jeep, stuff like that.
   and some we get feral trade - not just fairtrade but feral. trade unionists and others in solidarity bringing it back in their hand luggage. or nicaraguans on speaking tours of this country bringing the beans in their baggage. nicaragua, nicaraguita ... a nation of poetry, of poets despite all. i worked my balls off. fought 'em off ... and
   and a great silence descends in molotovs story. bootgirl rounds molotovs hands across her swelling abdomen, says
   if she's a girl i shall call her estralita
   - and if its a boy?
   bootgirl smiles, pulls molotov tight, tighter. the love she feels right now. so much love it hurts.
   - if its a boy? then mol.

molotovs happy hour

- you know i said i worked my balls off. fought 'em off ... well ... this aint easy. i was a virgin when i met all the estralitas of nicaragua. stayed a virgin. still am if you're asking. i didn't want sex, i wanted humanity. like you've seen, i fought my balls off literally. i've got one war wound. you saw it in the street. out there - nicaragua - it was raging, fierce. americans pouring in weaponry. we were one of the zones at war. the school and health-centre with bullet holes up their walls. we kept the terrorists away from the towns and villages for the most part, kept the terrors in the mountains. tried pushing 'em back. they would push up against us. one time they did – and i was right at the front. heard the safety catches coming off. knew what was coming. or thought i did. felt myself being hurtled back, crashing into tree stumps, branches, leaves. next thing i knew was i'd pissed myself. didn't know why. couldn't remember. thought it must-of been the scare. the piss kept coming. i felt weak. put my hand down. brought it up again. piss? my hand covered in red. it was blood. i sat there. cold. old. alone. the firing went away to my left. then more footsteps. i froze. but this time it was julia, commandante in our section. she dragged me away. others lifted me to a stretcher, carried me off that hillside. i remember a lot of jolting. fainting. in and outta consciousness. this field-doc stitching me up best he could. a lot of jokes were made about cojones. i was thumped on the shoulder a lot. i'd lost my balls, my ball-sac, my dick ... they stitched me up best they could. but the heat. and the lack of antiseptics. antibiotics. another thing to do with the american embargo. anyway my wound turned bad. green. pus oozed. i didn't really notice at the time. that's how feverish i was. couldn't piss. felt myself swelling up. began ranting. they managed to get me to the capital. managua. there was an international health team in. an international aid effort. they did the best they could, i was lucky. they cleaned me up by removing all traces of my manhood surgically, that's what was rotten. they made a great job. i have to take hormones all the time. whatever i am i'm not, no longer, a man.

   bootgirl hasn't removed her hand from molotov. she smiles into molotovs face. his beautiful dark eyes, black almost. and she says

molotovs happy hour

  - you'll never know how much fun a clitoris can be if you don't let me try

  they daren't move. not wanting the moment to change. bootgirl looks up at last, asks

  - these hormones you take? they stop you growing breasts?

  - something like that, something like

  she reaches up, squeezing one of molotovs nipples, adds

  - well. we will just have to see about that.

  hugging, holding, cuddling. there's plenty of time for bootgirl to take molotov to heaven. and back again. she wants his strong arms around. that night they want to sleep all cosied up like two beans inside the coffee-cherry. but first bootgirl says its time to share her story, only fair. know what they're getting into. open-eyed, not blind. as she begins to speak she looks into molotovs dark eyes, like wet wet slate. he's all eyes. and ears for what she has to say.

  - each and every morning i wake in pain. my left hand broken so many times the fingers are permanently crippled. this is just one manifestation of hate shown to me down the years because of my bisexuality. lived through hell - no metaphor - but a very real daily physical and mental grind in those cold north lands. punishment through primary and secondary, i was fair game. picked on, bullied, tormented. was kicked, punched, bitten, beaten, stabbed with pens, pushed down stairwells, had bones broken. i was 'lezzer', 'dyke', and a whole lot worse. even then they couldn't get the insults right. what is the correct insult for someone bisexual to the last twist of their d.n.a.? when this started, i was seven and didn't know what these words meant - nor did many my tormentors. never did get the 'rules' of kiss-chase – at eight refusing to chase the boys only but chased whichever boy or girl i was closest to. i still remember the teaching assistant on dinner duty grabbing my arm as i ran past, twisting it behind my back until i fell to my knees, scabbed up and crying, and then physically pinioned the rest of the dinner hour and banned from kiss chase thereafter. banned from kiss-chase for the rest of primary! the names and

molotovs happy hour

the fists and then the stones and metal bars carried on regardless. all the beatings sustained through childhood, torture during adolescence, future threatened when all i asked for was to be shown love. being gay hardly seemed the appropriate word for these circumstances. and i didn't know bi. one time left in streets after five men with metal bars attacked me and the police refusing to even investigate though they knew who the attackers were. punishment intensified as did the insults. as i got older the abuse worsened - every moment fear. years living more or less continuous with broke fingers, ribs, collarbone, other bones. bones broken methodically, in the streets, the underpasses, the playgrounds. this campaign of intolerance was aimed at my 'difference' - my questionings of assumptions around sexuality, my lack of comprehension over the 'rules', my flagrant disregard for my true feelings. i was attracted to the person not because of their dick or clit.

first chance i could, i moved as far away as possible. tried living quietly, slitting wrists, my stomach pumped. doctors and nurses never saw what i was going through as they forced that rubber tubing down, battering my throat, making me unable to give voice for days afterwards. learning the hard way what bi is.

i slept with men and with women, never falling in love. never finding that. when i was seventeen i thought i had pulled though. truly pulled. this was the one. i should-of known. she said you're a dyke. can see it in your haircut. can see it in your eyes. i said no. bi. she said crap. that's just your internalised homophobia. thought i must be stupid. i was infatuated. fixated. should-of seen the mania in her eyes. her political correctness crazying. wanting to make me un-bi. my lovers all have wanted a fuck or a lick, someone to suck their cocks or lick their clits but who then objected to my naming myself bi.

- you look a slut. honestly. look at you
- this is not how i dress. i am not given to such effort. but here i am. and all for the one woman capable of telling me to wear heels. bitch has stood me up for at least forty minutes – and this is dockside in coldcastle where

molotovs happy hour

crane-drivers, dockers, fisherfolk, oilies, come drink off their shift. and the men staring and i'm three inches taller on account of the heels - and i could kick, could bloody kick the bitch, knowing its deliberate. bitch chose this cos its her local, i had to bus it in, in three inch heels - how you supposed to run and kick in them? bitch chose heels for me - got them outta shoeshine - they did all the perv footing back there and then. they did motorcycle boots in firebird leather, they did crystal heels, they did ankle chain straps - with or without cuff loops to chain your wrists to. this must be love - a queercore kind, on which i'm musing, trying to make my bottle of metz last - and stay cold. mostly i switch off, staring into some private vision, on the hipness of two women holding hands in street, provided they're no actually sleeping together - its that old het-tease - men like looking at two pretty-girls but the moment anything looks queer ... and now through the door comes bitch.

  - you look a slut. honestly. look at you

and my eyes watering and bitch outstaring me just to see if i would cry, would actually cry. but i wont give bitch the satisfaction. momentarily, i look away. did tears happen? i turn back dry-eyed. give the coldest, hardest, longest stare. and then swinging for her. bitch legs it. i'm hoofing after her. one shoe twisted into a drain. i'm chasing woman up towards castlegate, almost gaining – even though i have handicap - one foot bare, the other in these ridiculous bloody heels. and i'm scream-scream-screaming at the one woman capable of telling me to wear heels. tore the other shoe off, hurled it at her hard as i could. next day i got a pair of purple steel-toe-capped d.m.'s instead. that's how i became bootgirl. whatever your sex, sexualities fine, but i'm bootgirl and i'm bi.

boots christened when i marched with thousands of others through the coldlands demonstrating against hate. attending vigils, remembering what i felt then, still feel it now. pride in who i am, in who we are. sadness at what the moral bullies of that nation believed me to be. i helped organise a delegation from the far-north – drove through the night to get to the demo, didn't sleep, demonstrated, drove back. on returning to the far-

molotovs happy hour

north – i found that we bisexuals weren't appropriate within the lesbian and gay societies. got thrown out of them too. their narrow-minded fearing we were threatening to some. we could be predatory towards the gay men. or dishonest with the dykes.

guess the thing about bisexuality is its harder to 'trap'. there isn't even a bisexuality singular; there are many - bisexualities, plural. all i know is for myself its not genitals that attract – i am attracted to the person. who they are. their mind. their caring. their love. yeah, i can have fun with whatevers between their legs but its not that. its them as person. love the person. though i am still nervous around people, find it hard to trust. and though i still wake to physical pain, permanent scars and am aware of the daily intimidation's around us i have managed it.

i have met so many young folk in pain and fear and isolation growing up as gay or lesbian or bisexual or transgender or thinking they may be ... know of some who have even taken their life because of pressure from the het-police. there are many more who have tried. why do the cold northlands live within their frigid coldness, their moral panic, their unyielding, unbending straight ways - why do they believe its acceptable to condone the bullying and the hate and the intimidation and fear? why don't they believe young folk should have access to information about their personal lives that will allow them to make such discoveries in a safe and supportive environment? why do they believe - whether we're gay, lesbian, bisexual, transgender, unsure or simply picked on because we don't conform – why should we be subject to campaigns of hate? folks out there - now - going through what i went through - they deserve, need support, just as i needed. country failed me, it fails them. though some of us may die and others suffer pain or fear, we will not be going back in the closet to appease those narrow views. if they had any humanity a clause outlawing the promotion of homophobias, transphobias, biphobias would be a good start. so yeah, you and me, me and you molotov, ... we've stuff in common.

how i left? rain was lashing eyes on leaving those coldlands, those northlands through vertical beads flung in head-on collision, the world

molotovs happy hour

refractory, awash, headlights swinging paranoia, believing any one of them filled with hatred for my tortured mind and fraught sexuality, would swing sudden off road, scatter fragments of my being dissolved in rain, self dissipated. had anyone cared they would have seen a crumpled silhouette more rubbish sack than human. had anyone been paying attention they would not have stopped but given thanks for their large car and solitude, shielding them from outside. within this storm i left the cold northlands, their narrow-minded morality junta behind, came south. my story, a common-land. so you and me both baby, you and me both.

   molotov is neither man nor woman. or he is both. together they are both. or neither. whichever way, they fit. they fit. molotovs saying yes to bootgirl, bootgirl saying yes to molotov.

   outsides been cleared up. meatman patched and despatched, though lost his days trading. police hammered on molotovs but he thought it politic not to answer. forensics will have taken photos of paw prints, samples of piss, but the piss will be too degraded for lab to tell which member of the feline family it came from. police put it down to hysteria. probably was an outsized moggie, making most of the chaos, don't want the local rag making some ridiculous fuss. remember all that silly season beast of bodmin from a few years back. eyes the size of lemons? no thanks. dog-walkers will notice the pull on leash as dogs dash past the place where the piss was spilled – but not understand the significance. bootgirl tries once more about the big cat - the black jaguar. molotov smiles.

   - you've heard there's been wallabies out in the peak district, a whole herd for years right up until recent-ish? beavers in east anglia. wolves returning to the highlands. dolphins in harbours all-over. scorpions marching on port-south. wild boars in savernakes and the new forest. big cat sightings on bodmin, yorkshire, northumberland. well my bet is unscrupulous zoo-owners, wacko millionaires, retiring magic acts have had all manner of wild creatures dumped when they outgrow their usefulness. what if some of these hide out. meet-up. mate. or cross-breed.

   i truly came across a wee black jaguar cub. up shotover hill. abandoned runt of the litter. someone had taken an air rifle to it for target practice. mother must have run, those that could keeping up, her carrying another in her maw. but this. this one. twisted and fell. then its survival instincts kicked in. burying itself deep in the thicket. the air-rifle morons couldn't get close. i used to walk around the lewis carroll nature reserve at dusk. could feel eyes upon me. this evening chorus lifting me, making me soar. and at first i couldn't be sure. but i found these scats. reminding me of out in nicaragua. i mean they were big cats. nothing else could-of laid 'em. and the smell, the smell! its something that gives dogs a jolt of primal adrenal fear. so i get down on hands and knees. try this undergrowth, stopping, listening, crawling. just an idea. and then i see 'em for sure. these eyes. like half-grown lemons. staring at me. unblinking. so i blink. keep blinking. its submission you see. lets 'em know they're top cat. the thicket they've crawled into is vibrating. sonic warfare. they release these subsonic rumbles to make their prey queasy. i'm feeling sick. but i sit it out. wait there through the night. blinking. not moving. stretching my arm out slowly. slowly. its not moving much. can see its wee. weakened. maybe ill or injured. take off my top. crawl in close. its shrugging further into the undergrowth. kicking with its good legs. growling away. but its running out of space. i'm moving in. but still i'm blinking. letting it know i'm submitting. until i get right in there. throw me top over. sink me weight down onto this snarling mess of teeth and claw but i've got its legs trapped, its held, can't move 'em, and i've got the neck pinioned just enough. poor thing. its fighting. but i'm trying to help. its weak. weakening. me own muscles are giving out. but it gives out first. becomes this pathetic sucking beast in me arms. manage to bring it back here a year ago. in a bad way. there was airgun pellets in its flesh. dehydrated. weak. couldn't-of eaten. so i scooped out the airgun pellets, lay there with it wrapped in an old blanket, disinfectant in its wounds. fed it milk through a bottle. mixed up scrambled eggs, chicken, fish – all de-boned. practically spoon-fed it. it was that weak. thought it might die on me. the first day i fed it drops of milk every fifteen minutes and wee nibbles of eggs, chicken, fish mash.

molotovs happy hour

didn't sleep. then the next day – the same only increasing it to thirty minutes. i was exhausted. had to keep resetting me alarm to keep me going. the third day we got up to hourly feeds and i knew it was gonna be alright. it was me that fell asleep. woke up to find the brute licking me. some kind of conditioning must-of taken place. thought i was its mam.

   the smell of its shite though. my god! i've taken it back to the hill many times. you saw her. she's filled out as much as she ever will but she's still runt of the litter, way smaller than full-size but way way bigger than a mog. she ranges far and wide. i walk up there. she stays in shadows the whole way. plus they climb you know. live up trees in the wild. let it forage for carrion and wild creatures on shotover. neighbourhood cats, dogs don't appear to go missing. she keeps in the shadows. there's been no sightings, no news stories, nothing suspicious – until now. i don't know. i think its time we did move on. time that we all moved on.

   bootgirl and molotov sit in friendly silence, until shadows lengthen, until dusk comes. until the first stars are out, feebly, above the light-haze of the south-east. they look out together. watch the stars. that night they both retire to bed in the cloud forest. and somewhere not so far-off, a pair of lemon-eyes keep watch until the morning star

lowlife

trades slack at molotovs with all the hammering either side. bootgirl works part-time to suit, but mostly its a case of keeping her belly covered, warm. keeping her head below the storm. she knows there a time to fight. and a time to wait. a time to fight and a time to wait. she does the rounds of charity shops, collecting for baby. her and mols wean. this kids gonna have them both for mother, candide for uncle – its gonna mess folks heads for sure. she checks out the window of oxfam for its special baby display; anything she could use? looks up to see these two collide in a clash of culture, a collision of classes. free entertainment.

woman coming out oxfam having deposited her unwanted while this man he's looking in, wondering whether there's an extra layer he can afford, he bumps into her and she knocks him down - elbows honed on years of little sister put-downs, end of year sales, riding lessons (the last horse simply wont do). its one those status things. plus, she's angry with hubbie for not coming in with her in first place, meaning she had to open doors and lug carrier bags when he should have done this instead of eyeing up the latest antacid cures and keeping the engine running .

- lowlife.
- if i'm lowlife. then you're a slag
- edward? edward! thump him edward. bloody his nose.

meatman leaps out the butcher-mobile looking for the ruck. meatman and our lady of oxfam have been dying to spill blood all morning. no contest. lowlifes down.

their engine roars them away as bootgirl comforts the flopped man and helps mop the blood down. man curls into doorway, blood down to his chin ... afraid to meet her eyes when she offers her last hankie. she must be on something or want something, no one acts outta genuine charity anymore. he don't know there are a precious few who will stop and help a

molotovs happy hour

stranger.
 once he's ok bootgirl heads back to molotovs. inside she finds this lass, nine or so practising her spelling. bootgirl imagines her own child-to-be. smiles. this lass with wacko uncle, some crazed anarchist, holding lasses right hand and smiling as she corrects her own spelling
 - ppp-i-ss- aa-rr-t-i-s-t
 bootgirl smiles. and it is then the baby gives its first kick.
 now storming the door of molotovs is transatlantic cousin of that rich-bitch oxfamista,
 - chop chop coffee to go. christ. get a move on. a move on. my coffee. goddamn
 she's been in the door like, all of 30 seconds, and still there's no steaming mug in her outsized american paws.
 - retards - this place must be full of.
 you noticed how americans don't really think except out loud? how their lips are always moving when they read the safety instruction cards on trains and planes.
 bootgirls similarly too loud
 - wouldn't serve her. she's obviously had too much caffeine already
 touristo glares. mol holds the door wide, ushers her out, shoots bootgirl a smile. bootgirl hackles and heckles
 - when you gets back to the u.s. of a tell your frequent flier friends to avoid east oxenforde. we don't want you clogging our arteries.
 the girl spelling out piss-artist is still talking away opposite her uncle. she's drinks down a peach teaser - ice, plenty of peach and a squish of lemon. and she talks and he listens and he smiles, smiles at her words and continues treating her as equal. he listens to her talk of radios and computers and friends and shops and holidays and school. and when she finishes her conversation and finishes her drink, only then does he say time to go? and she gets up to go and he puts an arm on her shoulder - a gentle arm, light and friendly and warm and he says
 - you know - next time i see you will be on the continent

molotovs happy hour

and she nods and so much unspoken. and as they reach the door she reaches out, arms around, hugging him close. he's got smiling eyes. and they well up. and you know what? she's got his eyes too.

bootgirl imagines her child-to-be being an equal like that. wonders what the first words out her mouth will be? bollocks? viva la revolution? i know my rights? she feels the pull of the tide inside and almost weeps. bootgirl heads for toilets, the babby weighing on her bladder. she washes her hands then cups the wee-one, before taking her place behind the bar. molotovs off for a riverbank wander.

boathouses smack bang right on the thames. if these were homes - you could house - street fulls, whole families to each floor of even the smallest. and how much is the land worth? how much if you were to convert these to houses? two million possibly. a whole rat-run of yuppies, only this being oxenforde we gotta row. molotov was in shadows as one of them on the south bank went up last week. building stood no chance - storing high flammables - something to do with boat building; and fire brigade couldn't get water - all that thames and no water; excellent. molotov don't carry matches – not his style, though he can't say he disapproves of what the arsonist did - but he does carry spray cans and he crept into the end of the smoulder spraying burnbabyburn and a large anarchist sign into the still hot art-deco bricks.

molotovs inspired by that godspeed you black emperor c.d. soundman handed him. before he even listened to its sound he loved that embossed cover, a diagram for a molotov cocktail. beautiful. and now on windows of molotovs a sandinista saying: only the workers and peasants go on until the end.

mol smiles at the thoughts of their babby, bootie and he. he sees a sequence of posters containing all the diagrams necessary for molotov cocktails. off the album cover and translated into english and as a series of posters, all the way from mandala way to pembroke street. spray kalashnikov up pembroke college; spray tupolev up kings college; ho chi minh up magdalen college. its a good deal more honest than taking the cash

molotovs happy hour

from arms dealers.

    that night bootgirl dreams she is looking in a mirror. the mirror is held in a cage of rib where her mother-flesh should be. slowly the shadow-reflect blinks and turns though bootgirl does neither. shadow reveals the delicate lines of the coldlands etched into skull, bare where hair should be, but the lines of her country, lives of her country aren't skin-colored - they are blood red. bootgirl in her amniotic sac of sleep remembering the blows, the shouts - babies are supposed to kick-out, instead it was feeling the blows as they laid into her, torturing marks out of her skin. that is why she fled. and why she will need to move on again. at least this next move she will have family, chosen, to keep her warm. she rolls, thrashes, sweats. molotov massages her temples. his hands smell of spray-paint still

animal farm

silt would consider his-self machiavellian if he could get beyond two syllables. instead he takes the e, the v, the i, and the l, please bob. he's on the prowl. he's watching the street, above all the beggar pleading just enough to score ... this one weaves beyond-drunk, eyes looking beyond - begging twenty pence for phone, his bus cards just out, his lass lost her purse, the puppy's starving: and the good touros and students meet his eyes, fumble and oblige. like as not you'll be clipped if you don't - run off down pembroke street - that's where the queen street cops sweep up the wallets, emptied apart from that telltale condom lovingly ringing the leather and so past its sell-by date

  - twenty pence mister? mister? borrow twenty pence for the phone?

  truth is he's homeless, driven out by the likes of silt - even landlord rachman turns in his grave - and north gate halls been torched again - but the oh-so-nice les-bi-gay-transgend committee - well, they're too too   liberal to accept anything other than it was another fag-in-the-paper-bin-accidental-moment-of-losing-it-passion, nothing deliberate, couldn't be that someone don't like the queers now could it ... and they are so awwffflly sorry for the inconvenience to the soup kitchen below - and they would donate leftovers from their kitchens, really they would, if only they could get over that whole health&safety thing; risk assessments no an easy country you know ... oh the liberalistas losing it so gently, genteely - and watch that beggar weave jaded, not even collecting the couple of quid he needs for night shelter, now he's got his twenty for the wrap of sweet relief brown.

  and there's a queue at the chemists. the ten past five snakyline waiting on methadone.

  - hey man. you just outta bed?
  - how did ya guess?

molotovs happy hour

- hard night was it?
- aye
- giro day aint for a while is it?
- nuuh
- oh man. what ya gonna do. sweat it out?
- i guess.

silt queues. he's waiting for amitriptyline. fifty milligrams. he likes to crush it small. sprinkle it in the fish tank. it keeps his catfish and his cichlids dozy. he don't like visitors watching his fish leap - it makes them jumpy and he wants them quiet, softened up.

in the queue, silt reads in the oxenforde times of a garden centre being destroyed by cacti fire. chilean cacti burst into flames regularly out in the desert and now in captivity. drier summers, global warming, low water pressure in the sprinkler system. he rubs his hands, he is that impressed. decides to send chilean cacti to all the properties on cowl road he's fingering, think of it as a kind of moving-on present. so much classier than calendars, baseball hats, pens. all the fuckers who are doing his head in how they will get torched by his cacti. molotovs first. christ, he hates that cunt.

silt moves forward in the queue. he remembers way back when. when he was a boy on a donkey ride. he felt sorry for that poor creature. big-eyes, flies crawling in. donkey flipped him off. he cut his foot. the man hit the donkey with a stick. silt grabbed the stick, beat the man. and bloody spain as he found later and their hobbling of donkeys, firing the knees with red-hot tongs, only a foreigner could do that. so he's given money to animal farm to collect donkeys from abroad. put 'em out to graze. silt keeps a photo of clara – his favourite in his wallet. best money he ever spent. the way she understands him as she takes carrot and apple from his flattened palm. claras worth every penny.

meanwhile the checkout girl on till number seven shop-and-go is seventeen and a lad. larry likes to dress this way. loves polyester uniforms. done up top-button tight to cover his undersized adams-apple. twice daily

molotovs happy hour

at breaks he slips out and into the bogs - shaves that upper lip - there's no hair anyplace else. and then slipping back and into the hairslides and platinum engagement rings of other checkout girls. conversations easy as last summer when that old wifey on aisle five hit the sun-lotion special promotion stand. she'd swerved to avoid a block of hayfever tablets falling. own brand the girls reckoned. and the results? a ten foot slick of factor thirty and wifey fracturing her pelvis. how they laughed, oh how they laughed

- she'll no be doing supermarket sweep unaided

they laughed buckets for weeks after, big yellow ones with handles and everything, choking, choking, each time the clean-up call came

- clean up in aisle five, clean up in aisle five

splutters of falsetto, tears of diet coke lunches busting their fine spray through noses. oh aye its a right laugh down these chemists, watching the human rats fighting over the last max factor. at night larry dreams he's dale wintons special assistant, his special girl, ringing the changes on condensed milk and asparagus soup and custard creams and cotton-buds, coleslaw and rich plum malt loaf, and, and, and ...

silts gonna open his new property-shop, his new office, end of the week now. its just about kitted out. now he's gotta find a supplier of chilean cacti quick. if molotov burns up that too bad, especially if he's inside. then silt can truly and lastingly clean-up and cream-up. upstairs a brothel – soon as he can get another boatload of vietnamese or other far-eastern lasses. have 'em working shifts. and a bright new jeep, no bloody brown stains on those seats

anarcho-psychology

- what we doing exactly?

bootgirl asks mol in the middle of the night, as gloved and hooded they enter silts property shop next door from the rear. molotov is careful not to crack anything, careful to move quietly, to not leave a trace. they've got painted scenery flats, buckets of quick drying paint, glue-guns, gaffer, nails. he's studied the psychology of colour and of shape. molotovs explaining

- anarchists in the spanish civil war used psychological torture techniques drawn from avant-garde art. the tricks they played with   colour, perspective, and scale. during the spanish civil war those anarchists they designed torture along these lines – distort or skew perspective, cause disruption, alter minds.

- and?

- were gonna fuck silts head.

- poor ash. what d'ya think happened?

- lets get this sorted first. we will find out where ash is. remember a time...

- .. and a place for everything. yes

- so we're gonna give silt and his dignitaries, his chums and the press a little working over. a kind-of uneasy listening on the eye. now lets cause confusion, lets sow a little mental distress.

they set to work in orange and black. lime-stripes. trompe-l'oeil walls receding, nailed in false floors, at all kinds of angles, but angles contrary to each other, angles to make you weep. colours that clash, enough to curdle any stomach. they've turned silts shop into a dolls house that even alice would see as wicked, an act of anarcho-psychology that will keep minds guessing which way to turn, even as they stumble and fall. they keep the lights off. its a full moon and they've got l.e.d. head-torches to help see their way round. in the dark a pair of huge yellow eyes keep watch. some-

molotovs happy hour

where around dawn they back out. finished
   what the fuck? silt unlocking at 8:30am. the foreman has handed over keys, having completed work the day before. meatman is gonna be spinning past shortly helping with the cacti: handing 'em out. little ties are around the cactis containers carrying silts most sincere and best wishes, his phone number and url. caterings due in half an hour - and in short skirts while the press are due at ten. foremans denying all knowledge.
   - this aint how we left.
   - paint-jobs like these don't grow overnight
   - i swear
   - cretins
   silt was supposed to be paying cash-in-hand. so he picks up the office stapler, and starts stapling fivers to the foremans flesh. foreman knows better than to interfere with silt when he's in a rage. he takes it like a man. keeling over when he can take no more. cracking his head open on a desk corner and spilling a pint or more of a.o. blood. meatman has to take him up to a&e – he's getting used to the hospital run. silts getting a splitting head-ache. can't breathe. he feels like the walls are falling in on him, crushing him, feels the walls are watching. he has to go outside for air. the catering girls complain of headaches too but he forces 'em back inside, telling them to set up the coffee and croissants, take their places. smile. greet the press. greet the local councillors. everyone else is running out puking paranoid.
   silt takes a claw-hammer to molotovs replaced window. hurls cactus after cactus inside. even silts backhanders can't keep this one quiet. councillors back-out. press depart abruptly. police haul silt off for quietening down. after they finish the croissants and coffee. outside. and molotovs had enough of this game. time to move on. him and bootie have been looking into heading way-out west, abertawe, starting afresh. take candide under their wing. and hunt ash down from the red republic. soundmans been in and measured up, wanting to expand pulse. he's looking for more space. there's still life left in the specialist indie record scene, especially

molotovs happy hour

mail-order and on-line. molotov will do just fine. he returns the cacti next door, stacks 'em inside when all the fuss has died down.

that night the cacti flame. molotov smells smoke around one a.m. comes down to find next door well alight. fire brigade are soon in attendance. they bring it under control some time after silts front window explodes, but well before the upper floor caves in. inspecting molotovs they say smoke-damage only. he can continue to live there but health and safety wont allow him to serve up food or drink. he tucks bootie back in, sits out the night and waits for soundman to open up. they got plans to finalise.

so's bootgirl and candide. he's getting better. he's progressing. his psychoses are coming under control. he's agreed to take largactyl in tablet form – 300mg in total, spread across six times daily. it keeps him under control but don't jitter him out, make him shake-crazy, he recognises her. above all he's keeping his mouth shut. as long as he does keep his mouth shut they think his psychosis is under control. in relapse. he's less gobby than he has been for weeks. should be getting section 117 soon. time off for good behaviour. bootgirl and mol promising to take good care, take him in. she's up to the hospital the morning to take in the chess-set he's requested, a pack of cards, some writing paper, fruit, decent coffee, see when he can get out. later she's got a pre-natal. then back to mols. eat. sleep. feels like its nesting time. she's had a beak full of twigs for so long, she just wants to sit back, feel that warm egg against her breast-feathers, listening for the cra-aack

molotovs happy hour

death by karaoke

ever watch a singer put their lips to a badly earthed karaoke machine? there you are down dancing preen and bam - 240 volts coursing through meatman, a right coronary shocker. shock-stopped, the on-screen words bouncing still. meatman and how he came undone in the presence of molotovs mate, soundman. it may just of been coincidence, though then again ... the possibility was of someone loosening some of the mike-head, unearthing the main power, running current the wrong way. whatever. serves the pisser right is what they reckon. meatmans had one too many cyclists beneath his bumpers, whole bars in uproar. they ended throwing wellingtons, riding boots, other rubber objects at him for fifteen minutes as he fizzed and crashed.

soundman remembers his own collision with meatman, the human-crusher last summer. six months on and his busted humerus still aches. the sizeable compensation from the insurance has finally come through for meatman crushing him and his bike beneath the wheels of his meat-wagon. compensation for broken arm and fingers and ribs - his humerus needed pinning, and psychological damage. compensation that's gonna be enough to allow him to branch out. pulse II in molotovs. who says its an ill wind? anyways soundman does remember how the ambulancemen refused to attend to meatman in case he wasn't earthed. death by karaoke. now that rocks.

and silts own demise – does it play out like some restoration comedy after police have given him a warning, calmed him down, told him he'll be court two weeks friday for criminal damage, contact his solicitor? was silts demise foretold in the collision of punts – the dunking in the isis – the finding that he couldn't swim? or the privatised bus shutting its doors on his silk tweetypie tie and dragging him face-down the road, turning rosemunds tarmac rosé with his bodys wine? the prick of one too many

molotovs happy hour

chilean cacti thorns – septicaemia going out of control? perhaps a tragic unskilled labor accident in cheap and shoddy buildmanship of another 'apartment' collapsing in on him in east-side as they're styling the oh-so-trendy zone before cowl? how about a mysterious accident with a french-fry vending machine - microwaving his internals until his heart busts out his chest? or slipping and impaling his-self on his mobile phone which vibrates at a frequency just so that his innards start to scramble in sonic warfare, d.n.a. unwinding back to nematode? or maybe a property-dig unearthing ancient anthrax spores and him contracting that. no. silt simply gets washed away as his namesake, re-deposited downstream - his body found by some dawn fisherman who calls it in.

the scene: iffley lock. dusk. a barge closing. some het-family on holiday, warring since they left banned-bury. that's a long time at four m.p.h. this is their stop for the night. tie-up here. no outside toilet facilities so they're gonna have to piss and shit and brush their teeth in that tiny enclosed narrowboat chemical loo. already their skin crawls at the thought of its chemikaze inevitability

- you steer
- no you steer
- you steer the bloody thing
- mammy, mammy
- what is it?
- there was a man there. and a black cat. big black cat. black cat pushed man in. now he's gone. magic. mummy.
- no.
- yes.
- no.
- yes.
- oh christ. oh christ.
- whats christ mammy?
- wheres the brakes? wheres the bloody brakes?
- put it in reverse. put it in bloody reverse.

molotovs happy hour

- i'm trying. i'm bloody well trying

oh silt - landgrabber, conqueror of watermeadows, parking lots, back alleys – his last word: glug and silt is now his namesake. that soft sound of a head being stoved in by several tons of holiday barge - its the sound of a cabbage being turned to soup. no soap opera though. coroner unable to do anything, apart from accidental death. there were scratches to his back, unexplained - was as if some big cat had swiped him but coroner couldn't put that down in his autopsy, who'd employ him again?

silt had parked his soiled jeep on mill lane. gone down to the weir to shout and scream his anger and frustration, to pound and rage, to expel that pain. decided to continue on for a pint now the anger was out his system. think on how to pull it all back. he crosses over far side of the lock intent on heading to the riverbank pub, get his mood back. he spots the field of horses on the other side. in among them is a donkey with the eyes of his own sweet clara. he's focused on her, not looking where he's going, gets too close the edge, then he feels an explosion at his back, black panther onto his scent, and he is wedged down the side of the barge, in the boil of water, several tons of rented barge stoving his head in.

silt enters his element, or it enters him, the muddy thames. the silt-slow choke of our harbours, our moorings, our docks. the slow silt choking them good. barge is tied up, conflicting witness statements given, a 'can you help?' sign put up on the towpath until some students chuck it drunken to the waters the following morning around three a.m. the families no use. pubs no use. of course there's no lock-keeper on. no-ones any use save the piping up of the child's voice. police nod their heads, uh-huh, uh-huh, bored. all cops can think on is fund-raising stunts for a life-size statue in bronze to be erected somewhere suitable for the anniversary of inspector morses death.

forensics? none. the body and suit once it is recovered will be immaculate, apart from a tear on the back, the head imploded, skin searched for anything out the ordinary. only thing that's found is that big cat pawprint scratch but it has to be hushed up, don't want more hysteria. accidental

molotovs happy hour

death. the first accidental act in silts life. c.i.d. find the photo of clara – silts beloved, his adopted donkey, when they search his body, and check through the wallet still lodged in his pocket. they're actually looking for a next of kin. all c.i.d. can find is claras address. animal farm. c.i.d. go round to the address on the postcard. this is how animal farm learns silt is no more. this is as close to next of kin as silt gets. and of course on death bank accounts get frozen. so poor old clara. no money now. how animal farm learns it is soon to be abbatoired, shut and cut. the animals rended and rendered down.

mol and soundman have shaken hands. deals gone down. first instalment of cash to help them move on and out. the rest to his account later once soundman is up and running in mols old shop. mols ordered ketamine – enough to stun a large cat, and a wooden crate. dealer thought it must be for his personal use. its not. where they're headed there's loads of space. a cat can roam hundreds of acres of sand, heath, moorland, mountainside even. there's deer, rabbits, fish, birds, for prey. mol knows a place of his ancestors outside sketty where they can crash. do it up. bootgirls made 'em all tortillas and avocado, and brings over great wodges of coffee cake to celebrate.

soundman even hands over a precious disc. talich quartet recording of smetanas first string quartet – from my life. one of soundmans favourite works. its special sound and soundman wishes 'em the very best. everything falls silent for the twenty-eight minutes of the quartet. then mol rises, passes round more brew, they raise their tiny pearl-black espresso cups, chink each others and toast the future, to freeing candide, moving west to the red republic and solving the mystery of ashes disappearance.

silts one remaining fan - a skin he commissioned to do molotovs in before he met his end brings a couple of cousins round to molotovs when bootgirl is up the ford-wars hospital arranging candides release. they shouldn't-of bothered. molotov ends up on trial for man-slaughter, he's pleading self-defence - seeing as there were three of them breaking in with tools of the meat trade and only one of him, unarmed. the fascist skins fell

molotovs happy hour

on their own weapons - the trial will determine how much molotov helped.

while on remand in bullingdon the fascist chums of the aforesaid surround him and get out their cocks, just to show whose boss. molotov sinks his teeth right in, taking the balls right outta the first, then slipping the balls into their mouth, forcing that man to swallow his own testicles. molotov hits back of the swallowers head hard, an explosion of teeth. once all is stilled molotov has a word in their ears

- i'm to stay unhurt, my friends are too, anyone i come into contact with is to stay unhurt. if this don't happen you will be killed like those others breaking into my caff with knives. you hear?

barely conscious they nod heads. on the landing, men step back. a screw starts to ask about the blood, molotov keeps head down, saying

- nosebleed sir. wasn't looking where i was going. sir

screw lets him pass. at mealtimes, seats are cleared for him. no-one asks what happened. four months down the line he will be cleared, self-defence. for now the prison library awaits this on remand prisoner. molotovs putting in requests for books by gerry adams, sergio ramirez, anton chekhov, angela davis, rigoberta menchú. who's gonna refuse?

prison medical revealed what molotov already knew. doctor asks about his missing meat and mol replies

- war wound.

he don't get hormones inside. but no-one comments on his chin, chest, back of hands all losing hair and smoothing over. nor do they comment on the swelling of molotovs breasts – like jeffrey archers gut, they put it down to prison stodge. mol looks forward to release and being reunited with his chosen family, seeing his wee baby estralita for the first time. the last scan revealing it was indeed a babbybootgirl, mol smiles on this and on the memories of losing his virginity to bootgirl. he lies on the top bunk night-times remembering her feline tongue.

mol sees bootie in bullingdon. they're allowed to hug. candides been refused permission to enter the prison, something about a potential breach of security. he waits outside. molotov tells them to take the takings. gives

molotovs happy hour

the combination for the safes lock. he tells them to head west. across the severn. hit the red republic. aim for the mumbles outside abertawe. put clear red water between them and oxenforde. they'll be alright there. safe. he's gotta stay fight a while but they'll meet him down the line. and then we can find whats happened to ash. he gives bootie the name of a top-doc in the red republic, tells how soundmans gonna drive the coffee roasting and brewing gear down, a crate too, at weekend. a ketamine laced side of sheep will put the big cat to sleep. it's all worked out. bootie knows the new address, she's got the entry keys. everything's been taken care of. this wee flat is his ancestral seat. a new country for them. mol returning to his roots, such as they are. he puts his hand under booties top, strokes her growing belly ... whispers he loves her. and how. she holds his eyes, says i know. times up. they part. mol back to his cell, back to his reading, his work-outs, his hormonal shifts, his body-change

molotovs happy hour

rebecca riots and riots

the red republic. molotov knows that with its history of labour and activism he fits. and now he feels able to return home, settle down with bootie and their bairn. soon as they let him out of prison. the red republic. a state of mind candide believes is right. the red republic. home to the rebecca riots, the merthyr and newport risings, the tonypandy riots. bootgirl feels comfy in all this. whispers to her daughter soon to be.

they're catching the late train west, it takes everyone through to fishguard and the boat out of the red republic and across the waters to another republic, ireland, around two a.m. though they'll have got off some three hours before. one last task, they've promised mol. candide keeps watch. bootie pulls out a large spraycan in raspberry pink, sprays down the arms dealer funded business school by the train station in the largest letters she can muster.

then they hit the train station, soon oxenfordes far far behind. the paint they've used clings tight. the arms-deal men have to bring in high pressure hoses to blast off the words. unfortunately too high pressure. they blast out the ink, pit the stone surrounding. so there's now a two tone wall. one that all those arriving at the train station can quite clearly read still.

- be thou the mother of thousands of millions, let thy seed possess the gate of those which hate them

its how rebekah spoke genesis, and its how the rebecca rioters spoke as they stormed the gates blocking their way.

and thirty miles north of carmarthen, newcastle emlyn - the first printing press of this red land, something especially admired by candide, or cee as he'd rather be known now he's out. rebecca riots. men dressed as women and causing rebellion, revolution in a petticoat - taking the ghost road, the coast road, the old road, riding unto the west. this is where it should be at, oxenforde twinned with ho chi minh city and carmarthen is managua

molotovs happy hour

spelt backwards, post-revolution. cee wishes his petticoat was ho-chi-mink and better starched.

- you taken your tablets cee?

bootgirl asks. rattles a pillbox in his face, makes sure he swallows. now he's out they'll reduce the dose of largactyl, bringing him down slowly, see how it goes, the trick is in not going cold turkey - that way will break him. instead a gentle easing off, and a general quietness from cee, no longer mouthing his thoughts out loud. for now though they tell tales on the train heading west for abertawe bay. telling what has never been said. and now and how. how it needs saying. slough off the old madnesses. gain some new ones. they are heading for the western fringe, beyond the military, the open-mouthed, the properties, the straight-laced, straight-faced, beyond the straightjackets. that's the plan. heading for that place in sketty where they can crash and rebuild. and they will walk the tides-line barefoot - as many miles it takes.

hunt the tiny welsh cowries - their wee white backs slipped in pink, hooked with the colour of skin. cee has vowed he will collect one hundred for each of them - drill the smallest most subtle of holes each end - as if a single grain of sand has bored through their ear - and he will thread them with silk, a slipknot smooth skein and they shall wear them all, one on the wall hung for ash – wherever he is. and they shall eat sea-salad all summer, coupled with chip butties from award-winning chippie we must go tend the garden: opposite the station. mols purchasing this place. he's gonna bring in espresso making steam, coffee bean roasting gear as well. and they shall all work there too.

they get in around midnight. fall asleep in a pile of blankets as they have so many times in the flight south. and now west. getting off the train they're amazed to realize that abertawe is one of the few cities you can truly see stars above, stars through. less light pollution. or maybe the backdrop of this place is painted that wee bit brighter.

cee can't wait to play the terrible uncle for estralita, or wee-bootie as he's already claimed, nicknamed. terrible-uncle: a combination of too

molotovs happy hour

many late night stories, midnight welsh rarebit on toast, piggyback rides, demented kazoo orchestras, a zillion teddybears, rolling down sand-dunes, and terrorizing librarians and museum attendants.

   that weekend they all see the same. mol from his cell, cee and bootie from under blankets. even ash wherever he's at. they see an image: neither waking nor dreamt. a large wooden crate deposited. a sleeping cat-like form, only huge, eyes like lemons, slowly waking, sniffing air, cautiously padding out. sand, sand-dunes, gorse moors, forest, moorland and mountain beyond. and a wee star bright, right above - estralita. one this shadow seems to follow and know

day-tripping

further west still for a day. tyddewi, the smallest of cities. walking on to saint davids head. rocks and surf and headland. bracken, cromlechs, ancient workings. sand and peace. the most amazing of stars. the babbys kicking regularly. bootie waddles, carries bottled water – fizzy cos of all the wind. carries cees tablets, he's not ready to drop them all quite yet, though they're scaling back. cee does what he can. bootie turns to him and says
   - i sheltered you in homelessness looked after when you feared the disintegrate. i fed you. anchored you within reality so you would not away. i soothed bruises, bathed cuts when you smashed hands and face to the frenzied pulp, stilled those voices calling, cajoling, threatening harm, promising nothing, asking nothing. i gave what i was capable. and you? you given me so much too - but why candide. why?
   - someones gotta be. i guess. and i don't wanna be me.
   - i understand. but no more madnesses hey cee. there's ...
she puts his hand to her stomach
   - i need you, need you like i've never needed you. you are my oldest friend.
   - aye three hundred years strong.
   bootgirl punches a smiling cee who rubs his arm. the baby kicks. the tide off saint davids head sweeps all before. cees clocks about unwound. he's ready to let it out. let all out. cee cracks. feels his personality pulled apart. feels his-self crumble, crumbling, like sand ripped by tide, like rock ripped by the surge of wave, of waves piling in. bootgirl waits. at last
   - i was never candide, always cunegonde, thinking i wanted to lop-off that extra length. this was for years, until i realized it wasn't cos i longed to be woman, it was cos i hated my prick. learnt to love - or at least tolerate it. i allow it took time - and love? - don't know that i do, though   other

molotovs happy hour

men seem to love it and woman tolerate ... it was that spurt, the growth of it i couldn't handle. it was that word. that four letter word. the one worse than cunt or fuck. love - the original four letter word. love - those four bastard letters. candide lived that volt may die. that volt may-of died. i fell. fell hard. fell far. for volt. v. friend. lover. confidante. comrade. my other. volt was everything you know? this is me telling it best as i can. me telling the only way i know how. i kind-of unpicked it in the hospital, kept it quiet, its not for the ford-wars to hear you know? though there was a decent nurse there. someone explained psychosis to me. somethings get locked up kinda funny in memory. find the key. those large orange pills – they're no answer but they helped still me enough to provide a key. well ... volt. he ... he ...

how the smell of rubber is come to be sex though really its a kids party, balloon-popping, the thin rubber tears laughing ... someone elses past, make of it what you ... the well of the spiral-staircase below edgecity gallery and its café half full of white balloons. its half filled with white balloons, the smell of rubber in the air, truly. its art. and it invites. and pushing your way in and through and feeling disorientated, a little scared, or give in to the pull of rubber, laugh at the hystericalness of all yesterdays parties, even though they may not be yours? what d'ya get off on? ankle boots, glitter-dust i never could resist (they say inside every bi-lad is an essex girl screaming), neon flash of some impossible clubbers jewelling hung from neck - and the smile, that smile - pure kid. but ankle-boots was what i saw first, until the balloons shift, face emerging, and then the neon. can't remember what s/he was wearing but i remember this is art. gallery. and they say the word ars means art, and i'm horny, wanting.

i'm loving this mess of balloons; wanna fuck among the laughter of it. and volt and me having a ball and losing ourselves in the laughter of it, losing yourself in the balloons, losing yourself in the rubber not of sex, but of play, of childhood, of a childhood we neither of us had. this is how / where we connected; our connecting; wicked wicked lip-licking looks. and then our busting of balloons as v bent over railing, giggling, and no

molotovs happy hour

one seeing though they so easy could as we fucked in half the given space - that was the title of this artwork in the gallery. half the given space- a sea of balloons, the swelling tide of rubber occupying half the given space and the curators above, pleased that art was being enjoyed judging by all the bursting, and us revelling in the lust of it, the sheer exhilarating thrust - and no we didn't use rubbers, there's still some stuff to which we cling. those days were honest. txting when we needed to shag, anytime of day or night, the two a.m. knock saying i need. we killed time together and in the doing slaughtered that gaudy neon angel hovering high above our edgecity. and we took the magic that was edgecity at night, best-time for our sprawl of city, coldness sweeping away the day and striking up, lighting up a fiery delight; the hallucinatory cross past law-courts; the salvation for all; the majestyk racists; the cheese-pastie assistants; naked flames; bare-shouldered lasses burying the capital of north financiers; skateboard kids looking on through henry moore and all the while plaster saints on high, high above are drinkers from long forgotten pubs immortalized, their busts where most folks don't gaze. and above even this; the regeneration cranes building a twenty-four hour city - though mostly for those with twenty-four hours to wait. glitterdust and neon - that's edgecity. cheap cheap glitterdust, and still it makes us throb all the way. and i know i've said this before but it still stands why are the only women i fall for are dykes or men? what this say about me? but volt is part of the story. what chances for a transsexual who's never been further than the m62 and edgecity? everyone else we ever screwed wanted something, but s/he wanted only my balls and cock and i wanted above all to eat that perfect sculpted place. perhaps the surgeon loved women, or hated men, or been hated by them, either way we fitted. volt mouthing honey i've lost some meat. and i reply honey: we've all lost meat along the way. we've all lost some meat.

    but: all too soon - evening closes, an autumn sort-of way - i feel the chill though its still summer nights, just. the onion bread pounded, kneaded, risen again. its smooth elastic giving a harder shell. and that smell of bread!

molotovs happy hour

of oil and birth and redemption. and the peppers sweated ready and cream soured to volts favourite goulash thickness and the sound of her keys no rattling our door and the phone no calling out; and i'm spitting sweat cursing why don't she ever wear that watermelon watch i gave and tears down my face.

    knowing her clocks no wound to our tight-sprung world and i check the telephone, rub pad into its cradle just to make sure it really is connected and it is and i pour jack daniels to the back of my throat; feel nothing; pour more ... until the flood. and the bread pound-pound-pounded, the onion bread, volts special recipe, the onion bread we shared in the pound pound pound oil elasticated skin-sweet smell of cumin, of thyme, of chopped black olives, pound pound pound, the bread pounded, risen, and hunger rising and the bread left to go hard as we ate each other without cutlery. tears down my face pound-pound-pound the frustration/s of bread so well pounded it doesn't even stick to my fingers and i refuse to be bound to volts timetables. why doesn't she come?

    we discussed a surreal circus and bread burglary - how volt would, really would, bust into someones house when they were gone, cook a perfect three courses and leave this for their return, timed just so, candles still lit down to the perfect sculpture of wax. we used to imagine there must be gideons atheists sneaking into lonely hotel rooms late at night – leaving slaughterhouse five or catch 22 or the joke just to mess with lonely minds.

    hands to eyes i rub knowing i shouldn't-of, now the onion blinds memories of volt. then from far off - the sound of sirens, closing. i know they're headed for me, heading for me. then the black-jacket and silver-tongued police officers knock, their rehearsed

    - please take a seat. we have some bad news. volt passed away. she took a beating. we will do all we can to catch the aggressors. is there anyone we can call. would you like a sweet tea?

    and the bread risen to a perfect state, but i cannot bring myself to swallow

    that's how it was with volt. this gorgeous human, i fell in love, fell hard.

volt gave me candide. the book. volt gave everything. and then volt was gone. killed. i fell. fell apart. v's book was the only thing i had of hers. came to believe the book was me. its like the whole story is true and only the author is a figment of imagination.

    bootgirl pulls candide – her oldest of friends – close. they hold one another tight, watch the three thousand miles of ocean roar, thunder, crash.

    - call me cee. he says. call me cee.

    welcome back cee. the largactyl is to be lessened and finally lost in cees battle back to a more mundane reality

still beating

molotov behind bars. not for much longer. his trial will find him so-oo not guilty. soundman has delivered his post from the shop. nestling in there is a photo, a view so familiar, this folk mural on the walls: one of the few left over from the sandinista revolution: and winged beings, winged folk, feathered beings stretching their labour and their redemption alongside the non-winged. its the folk mural photo molotov gave ash. its the card ash must have sent from his new destination. the reverse reads
   winging it all the way from there to here.
   with a miniature drawing of england and that central american isthmus so familiar, a tiny broken thread of line.
   ash has somehow made it through to the other side. molotov is delighted. that picture is tacked up beside his top bunk. no-one will touch it that's for sure. when bootie turns up with her eight month bulge for one last visiting hour he shall hand it over, explain all he knows.
   soundman has bought out molotov. he needed a bigger place, a bigger space. he's given fair price, they've shaken and soundmans moved in, closed the other one down. its now called pulse II, it does records, tapes, c.d's, coffee, chocolate, benefit gigs. molotov using the cash to set up home with bootgirl and c. new future in the red republic. over the door of pulse II is a neon green pulse beating. still beating. still fucking beating. yeah. molotovs going to have a pulse beating just the same over his own new coffee shop cum chippie we must go tend the garden once he is released

molotovs happy hour

part 2. those of you seeing an angel not realising it could just be a hyperactive firing of the visual cortex

overhead strain to stay airborne that rr-rr-oa-rrrr, the skyfill with noise like english hornets, helicopter coming, the burst of white thundering eyes. why does the airspace overhead use ash as the turning point for their circling?

*

it might be only dancing but down corridors that moorland asylum it looked for all the world as if ashes shadows took flight. when ash told of his secret wings, candide didn't blink once. ash lighter than whipped cream that candide can taste but can't lick, touch. how ash shared his great winged secret and candide did not blink once. comrade

*

dancing is ashes escape from the here and now - place he's little in common with and less love for. this he recalls as the angry buzzing, mad hornets, helicopter sounds, stun grenade hitting him full on, no time to vomit, the world a million miles off, ears exploding, he faints

*

like dancing boots you haven't worn in, oh, so long, and your feet slipping back in a natural; that's how ash always imagined wings would feel; that

molotovs happy hour

feeling. ash has always had that pull at his back

*

ash coming around on garage floor. someones standing on candide. hard. candide cant see, must be unable to hear, nothing ash can do, whoever these are, they mean business. ashes back is itching so bad under his long trench-coat. can feel the tremble of his wings. their ache. that. he's hauled out to sky-black helicopter which blows grit on those holding the perimeter below. ash thrown up and into this helicopters belly. ash pinioned in a five star to floor. they cut all his clothes off. even his beloved leather jacket. a photo of a nicaraguan mural falls to the deck.
   - what the fuck?
   this anti-terrorist corporal screams on seeing ashes wings. his c.o. slaps corporal in face
   - this scene did not occur. this scene did not take place. this scene does not exist. understood soldier?
   - ... yessir ...

*

moth in bath. ash desperate, trying to rescue. somehow it winged straight into the water. mams away with it, in her rocking chair. he's looking after his-self. he usually does. meal-time. bath-time. night-times. tonight this moth blew in through open window mam was sitting at, watching the flares and gas and cooling towers, his smoke-monster town. moth wont climb on his fingers. if he tries picking it up he will squash it for sure. a piece of toilet paper. quick and under. paper turns clag. this silvery wing-powder on top. moth dead. ash cries. he puts paper and moth to dry out beside radiator. come morning, the moth feebly flutters. is this wind? or his breath? again it flutters. he holds out his finger. moth flutter-flaps onto it. just where he has this cut from stone thrown at the boys who call mam

molotovs happy hour

names. moths tongue unfurls. it unfurls like bracken! tongue tickles. how it tickles! moth distils its moth-juice into him, direct, via the cut. there, a wee sparkle iridescent as moth-powder, wing-juice, takes flight, a spark of molten ash under his skin

*

american and english voices blur in the dip and tilt and chase of helicopter. bug-eyed soldiers pinion his wings. tree-tops whip. birds tip from their roost. the occasional swivel-head hoot – owls from dark. blanked out goggles over his eyes. blanket thrown over. then the pinion increases. flat to his stomach, face to one side, recovery position, naked, this means they don't want him dead, yet. nothing audible above the hurl and shriek of blades, the chattering of his teeth, the clatter of coded communications. helicopter banking, plummeting, blades subside, they have landed. manhandled. guesswork from beneath his blanket and blindfold. then some liquid-soft mush pushed against his lips. he swallows greedily. then a water bottle to his gob. again he sucks greedily. sucks for more. then gobs it all over them, his best water fountain. boot on his nape. for a long time he is cold

*

  – hey wee angel, don't get so frightened. its ok, look
  and mam points up at the clear cold sky
  – statues with wings. see? sshhh. i go flying with them some nights. and so beautiful. they wont abandon us. keep looking. you might see a shooting star. its really one of them coming to help.
  mam traced wings against his back with fingers so gentle they felt more like feathers. ever since that day he felt the place where they sprouted from. could feel his little baby-wings there, a presence invisible to all but him, waiting for the right conditions to sprout and grow. a knot inside his mus-

molotovs happy hour

cle, bone-deep, lifting his shoulder blades up, up, up. so that's where mam flew when she wasn't in her rocking chair!

*

wings mould the brain. neural mapping of new body parts. wings moulding a new mindset, wing-set, a winged brain. pain and re-imagining, the two horizons between which all experience - human / winged / other - must exist.

   cyborg-envy, implant avatar, this angelic bastard remoulded. pain and re-imagining. sweet future watchers, blue-sky thinkers who believe somehow the cyborg to be future ageless, sexless, chrome-sleek deathless. fuck that. here is the spreading-glorious, a must for experimentation, winged soldiers, now there's a trick you don't want to miss. m.r.i., p.e.t., resonance scans reveal the implausible within. ashes bones are indeed hollowing – the structure like a birds – the same honeycombing – how is this possible? he should be falling apart. his body rotting. instead he's never looked or felt so good. so light. above all how can the military-industrial exploit? how can't they? who wouldn't want winged soldiers on their side? the young military medic whistles in wonder

*

butterfly kisses mam calls it. and she bends in close, tickles ash on his forehead with her eyelashes in rapid opening and closing. she opens, closes her eyes fast as a butterfly wings, all soft, gentle, soothing, butterfly-like, and he falls asleep to this rhythm, these little wings

*

   - those of you who saw an angel not realising it could just be a hyperactive firing of the visual cortex. science has explained too much light, some

molotovs happy hour

eyes don't cope haloing in / out, the result - well that's all there is to angels but you ash, you

    this young medic whistles, stirs his instant coffee, ash wishes he could have some of molotovs brew. he wants to think on his friends but in here, this place off the map, the battery of tests he has to endure, alone. text subject gx-zero-5. they refuse to call him ash. at least they gave him back his photo. its now bootprinted, but still viewable are the folkmurals on the walls: one of the few left over from sandinista revolution: and there, winged folk, a peasant version of bosch or chagall, stretching their feathered beings. is it in the air or in their brew?

*

too soon they took mam away and ash wasn't allowed to see her. they said hospital would be better. her last words
    - no bars on my windows or how will i fly?

*

the young military medic is trying his hardest to understand through the battery of tests he runs. still unsure on the language
    - and how long have you had those, er, um ...
    - wings, they're called wings
    - and how long you, you know ...
    - they're called wings

*

one day ash is taken aside. told there is no school that day. he's told mam jumped to her death off a waterfall. she'd gone out there in a fierce storm, pushed past others who were turning back. she wasn't wearing a coat. the strange part was no-one saw her fall nor could they find the body but reli-

molotovs happy hour

able eyewitnesses say she jumped, jumped in for sure and though police posted a watch downstream the body was never caught ... ash smiled then because just for a moment an image as sun came out, this ghostly apparition, hovering then disappearing: his mam. they wrote down furious notes about him smiling at this. but what's the point in crying when she's flown, escaped them all?

*

slices of his mind on the scans lit-up like christmas, inside the tube of their machine and they are all racing, racing
   - remarkable. quite.
   how our memory becomes winged memory – our memory capable of expanding to cope with new experiences. new networks, new neural pathways, adopting to the new information, new sensations, wingtips, leading to a new mind
   - fascinating. just fascinating
   ash wants out of this tube, their machine

*

one day finding a swift on the ground. aren't they supposed never to land? nine, and he so gently cups that bird to hand, looks deep into and through the eye, its heart stilling from initial fear. places swift in a box. tucked away where no-one can find. a wee bed of straw. goes and grubs up a worm for din-dins. returns to an empty box. perhaps a local cat got the bird. no evidence of feather-scatter though. ash would like to think it flew

*

   military medic tells ash
   - we only use ten percent of our brains. they say the other ninety percent

molotovs happy hour

is vast, unknown, perhaps unknowable. dolphins have helped sailors back to land. lions have nursed the abandoned antelope. jaguars stun with a subsonic roar. pigeons migrate via electro-magnetic fields, a tiny liquid layer in their eyes; and swallows can locate a single spot twelve thousand miles away. penguins stand on ice for months just to keep the egg from freezing. whales echo-locate others across oceans, singing a subsonic song of millennia. and whales have been known to beach themselves on sharp rocks, committing suicide, when their mates song is switched off. whales kill themselves because their songmate is silenced. species die. species survive. and you - are you surviving or dying? which side are you on?

*

this gunning of engines, squealing of brakes, rubber, metal as two cars race for a gap for one. and then, ... in that time of silence before the crash, that one perfect moment of stillness before the explosion – something miraculous: they say that birds are quiet before the storm. here in edgecity the starlings that hang around this ex-graveyard startle. take off. swarm every-which-way - for a moment forming a question mark mid-air; thousands strong. a private viewing. and again ash feels the tugging at his back. by now no mam to tell all to and be soothed and butterfly kissed by. ash in care, has to keep his winged thoughts locked, only for moments like these when he is not watched, not watched at all. his skin itching ready to burst wings but the time is not ripe

*

ash is eye-deaf / ear-blind to the thin fins of light on a military runway in the shire surrounding oxenforde as they stutter and light. this is where he has been brought after the battery of tests are finished. the young military medic said something about making a soldier of you. everything is hush-hush. they refuse to address him by his name. and here at the military base,

molotovs happy hour

beside the runway a different roar. big engines these. like bass notes of cathedral organ. surround-sound. this structure he has been handled into vibrates with them. he cant see a hercules in final flight check. he can feel though, his whole body feels, his wing-tips testing that wind, he is so near flight. but still pinioned

*

fearful of future disaster, ash keeps watch. there's a turning circle for planes right over his edgecity estate. some beacon signal that sends the flights on their way or gets them to alter course, something is broadcasting co-ordinates. ash has to focus all his mental powers on keeping those aeroplanes up there. and once he does the planes settle into a rhythm, staying airborne, turning left, right or straight-ahead just as ash in his head-messages describes. he works hard, naked to the elements, because this is how he broadcasts best. police disagree. moorland asylum disagrees. fuckwits. some kinda magics gotta keep them from crashing, its not as if he hears voices, sees things that aren't there, no! he always feels the pull of wings, something at his back tugging, like a nagging toothache that wont be denied. he needs to take off, soar, fly. he's become skeletal, feels so light, like his bones are hollowing out, ready to take flight

*

giant black form of hercules struggling to gain air, to take flight. there's a moment in these planes when all feels doomed, they surely weigh too much? more thrust defying law, laws, natures law and order. inelegantly plane forces itself off the ground, screaming. airborne proper at last. its flight path on military radars. all civilian flights are moved off its co-ordinates. there's a clear path all the way to the bristol channel, any altitude. and beyond. way, way beyond

molotovs happy hour

*

least he has a comrade in candide. candide nods sagely as ash tells of averting near-tragedy one night, some bloody metal monster barely airborne coming in right on his floor and out on the balcony his clothes abandoned as ash desperate, sending head-messages out with all his fervour for the plane to lift, to stay airborne, to turn to the east - and it does! candide tells ash that fox-hunting should be licensed - but only for inner-city areas. lets see those redcoat fuckers hunting and hurting after urban foxes and the working class jeers of edgecity. hunt is after all rhyming slang

*

hercules aiming for a cruising altitude somewhere above civilian flights. ash – ear pop – sucking for scarce oxygen; his body beyond cold. over lundy the new, long haul co-ordinates are confirmed, west south west, a long long haul ahead. heading for the former british colony of belize where law is lax, relaxed. belize, school of americas, guantanamo, kenyan highlands – venues like this right across the developing world, where the military can experiment without interference. venues way beyond the probing lens of international law

*

ash is for one night coated in moth, coated in moth that one night, their blur ahead of storm off moorland and into hospital. that's when the pendulum swings to the other side. his wings burst from skin and start struggling and striving and stretching for air. later candide will place a long black trench-coat around the shoulders of ash, smile at him. the coat has an impossible airiness and lightness and space, something he can grow into. candide whispers to ash
   - in my three hundred years i have seen many things

molotovs happy hour

and strokes ashes back, traces the outline lightly through his long black coat

*

ash, airborne, even as his wings are bound. he is not in smokemonster where mam traced wings on his back, he is not in edgecity where the moors brought moths that clothed him and winged him, he is not in oxenforde where he was among friends until the rip to military and those arduous tests on his wings. he is in this aircraft, heading out across the atlantic. a bottle is placed against his lips, and greedy, hungrily, he sucks at the mash, the slop. a voice, midatlantic says
  - whoaa, careful there soldier.
ash tries moving his lips, they mumble, stumble, tries to shape
  - soldier? my name is ash. where you taking me? what's going on?
brusque replies
  - you're a soldier now. you're on the side of right. of justice. everything else is classified.
  the cover over ash is replaced. night falls whenever the master orders it, like an expensive talking parrot in its cage

*

now ash keeps his clothes on tight. refuses to take them off in that moorland asylum. they keep on at him to strip, to bathe, to change clothes. and all through this they keep watch. they want to perform a physical examination. ash holds them off long as he dares. until the inevitable physical they take him off for where ash refuses to lift top further
  - and what are these scars?
  - stretchmarks
  a long pause.
  - i see

only they don't. ash has become skeletal, feels so light, like his bones hollowing out, readying for flight. psychiatrist forces the issue.
- why keep yourself so wrapped up? why keep your clothes on tight? we are all friends in here. let me examine you. why wont you let me examine you?
ash is forced to reply.
- because of my wings.
- your wings
- aye, my wings.
- you say you are winged, that you have wings, so lets see the proof
ash takes off his long coat and there in the moorland afternoon light, he stretches his wings.
psychiatrist crumples into the corner, whimpers and cries like a puppy that has pissed itself. ash tries talking to the psychiatrist but there is no language where the psychiatrists belief system has been so spectacularly burst. psychiatrist is admitted to his own ward where he spends afternoons crumpled against radiators and whispering impossibilities about wings

*

ash lying in his cage on the airborne hercules dreams up furiosity. as he does the plane experiences turbulence. hits a hellish patch of air over the gulf of mexico. they've already diverted northwards on account of hurricane warnings over the caribbean. the plane bucks, broncos. is ash having this effect? he lays off and plane stays steady, ash fires up and again the plane bucks. this is him, his effect, the effect of his wings. he is a moth stomping and stamping and it is having an effect

*

- we gotta escape this hospital. there's an eighteenth century city - oxenforde - to hang out in. get a couple of periwigs, keep your coat on, blend

molotovs happy hour

right in.
    candide keeps his word. they fly south. oxenforde. the garage. molotov. bootgirl. voltairechoruses. keeping his long-coat on. learning from molotov there's a time and a place

*

nows the place, nows the time. the hercules transporter plane is trying to work around cuba, around the hurricane, then loop over yucatan and head for the landing strip south of belmopan, southern belize, close to the guatemalan border. these are places off the book, off-record, off maps, there is no accountability there. military can explore anything they like - even winged soldiers. ash thinks of all the planes he has kept aflight, thinks this is the one to down. again he surges cacophony from his mind and again the plane responds, immediately hitting extreme turbulence. everything tossed like so much seaweed flung high on a storm tide. a soldier comes back to check he is tied down tight. ash asks
  - where are we headed?
soldier says
  - where we're headed is classified soldier
  - but i'm ash. not a soldier
  - not any more you're not. this takes priority
  - but
  - listen: less you know, the less you can be harmed. alright? ... you wont have any complaints soldier. just do as you're told and you'll be treated fair. we're all working for a higher power, a greater good. you wouldn't believe what weapons we are facing. we need anything that can give us edge. you're that edge soldier, you're that edge.
    aeroplane has crossed yucatan, has worked around the hurricane now, its over belize, altitude lowering towards belmopan, heading for the top secret military base to the south. its now or never, ash, now or never. ash cooks up the fury, furious, unleashes the turbulence of his mind. instantly

molotovs happy hour

the plane bucks, thrusts, thrashes, sounds worse than a ship whose propeller comes out-of water on the biggest waves, ashes restraints snap. he can sense red lights, panic, communications storm, static and energy crackling through the air. ash crashes his mind and thoughts together again, wanting only to down this plane, even if it means ending him. he dreams up a storm, calls forth his fury, and like prospero, spreads his wings, raging against the injustice of it all.

plane has no time to put out a mayday call. it is loosened like cigar leaves unfolding, then hurled. a brief radio report on the six o'clock news reports only that a military aircraft carrying a top-secret anti-terrorist payload was lost in mysterious circumstances. there are believed to be no survivors

*

ash regains consciousness in the top branches of a tree where he glided to, away from the bucking of a holed plane. his wings held him, his wings actually held him! now its dusk in the tropics. below the wreckage is all around. helicopters wasp, low voices all american, crackle of communications. ash stays tree-top hidden as ground search look then leave. moths have again clothed him. these are huge. tropical. must be 12 inches wide, maybe more. he collects moisture off leaves with his fingertips, offering this to the unfurling proboscis which drink. the moths they clothe him. this hides him from the search of soldiers. he remains in forest canopy until search is called off. moths cloth him, hold him, enfold him. never has he felt so held, so warm, so close. during nightfall, a shooting star. he notes its distance, direction. in the morning this will be the route he treads

*

scratched. scraped. barefoot. living off forest. forest living off him – he is ecosystem too for the slow leaching of blood and bone, making him so lean. he hardly needs food these days. his wings feel stronger too.

molotovs happy hour

losing track of the days, thinks he is following the passage of the shooting star. south-south-east. he crosses borders known only on maps. he drinks the forest. eats the forest. listens and lives the forest. the forest lives him. his hearing is acute. can hear sounds beyond the human reach. cocks his head to one side, like a thrush listening intently. then he moves on. ash is experiencing a new world, a new life, feels he is out of his cocoon, and so alive

one night he breaks above cloud-rainforest, a bare cone of volcano. he continues to follow the passage of the shooting star. he smells the changing smells of leaf and plant. it has been two weeks, more, when he finally leaves thick cover, approaches smoke, habitation, daylight. on top of that volcano around dawn he descends through cloud-forest, beneath el tayacan trees, through coffee plantations. untouchable is how he feels

*

fuck! how everyone smiles and claps when they realise he's for real. a wee child reaches her tentative hand out to stroke the wings. shrieks as they tickle her. nothing needs saying. ash points at the mural of this poor village in the segovias, in the north of nicaragua. nothing else needs saying. ash has a winged brain unlocking new neural pathways, the live synapse, as info flows – light and breezy.

this village in northern nicaragua where all kinds of life are lived out. all kinds of human flotsam and jetsam ended here. the north-american flagpole painter who should-of died falling from that height, but didn't – instead realising he was on the wrong side, fled south and here he is. the body-artist who chopped off her little finger and painted slogans with the blood until they shipped her out from colombia. the russian poet who speaks only whistles, clicks, hums, like dolphin sonar. the south african sisters conjoined only at one hand (three hands between the two of them) who fled, refusing an operation, easy by any standards, but wanting to stay combined in that way, wanting to stay that spectacularly in touch. all those

molotovs happy hour

the first world would refuse or refute, those labelled, the fighters and the poets, they gather here, refuse the labels, accept ashes wings. they make room around the fire, sink the local brew, roll a few, listen to the music of the forested night, the unbelievable sounds.

ash smiles so intensely feels his face is cracking. they pass more brew. how come people with next to nothing are so willing to share what little they've got, put a stranger with wings up. accept him into their life, smile, play their version of the guitar, sleep, see another day.

and that folk mural still on their walls: one of the few left over from the sandinista revolution. winged folk, a peasant version of bosch or chagall, stretching their feathered beings alongside the non-winged folk. ash points. they smile. nothing else needs saying. he will give them what he can, work alongside, flexing and stretching. the bricks and mud of this village for canvas and the people shall dance and sing and grow and be given wing, aye, given wing. ash writes a message on a scratched, battered photo of the mural. addresses it to molotovs, cowl road, oxenforde to let them know he is free at last. ash don't know yet but soundman will pass it on to them safely. compañero, compañera, circumstances happen, things occur, we can change